RUFFIAN IN WAITING

By James Murray—

Novels

The Pale Sergeant
OlympiAntics: A Factasy
Shark City

Short stories

The Bulletin, Town Magazine, Australian Short Stories, MJ Magazine

History

Phoenix to the World: Sir Raymond Purves and Clyde Industries
Lifework
Alcatel Australia: The First Hundred Years
The Woolworths Way
Beds, Boots and Backpacks: Y.H.A. Australia (co-author of the latter with John McCulloch)

Documentaries

Gold, Silver and Bronze: Australians at the Olympics
The Portuguese Discovery of Australia
The Last Trek (writer/producer with executive producer Ted Morrisby)
Olympic Glory: The Golden Years 1896–1972 (writer/producer)

RUFFIAN IN WAITING

JAMES MURRAY

ARCADIA

First published 2017 by ARCADIA
the general books' imprint of
Australian Scholarly Publishing Pty Ltd
7 Lt Lothian St Nth, North Melbourne, Vic 3051
Tel: 03 9329 6963 / Fax: 03 9329 5452
enquiry@scholarly.info / www.scholarly.info

ISBN 978-1-925333-61-9

Cover design: T.F. Mirabello

To the memory of my brother
Daniel Murray, A soldier
The Highland Light Infantry, Palestine
The Royal Australian Regiment, Korea
Born Glasgow, 1928. Died Adelaide, 1960

Prologue

Fire: the present consuming the past, the thought drifted out of the walled garden, drifted on a wind from the west into the mists of Connemara as a cloaked and hooded nun fed leaves onto the fire, leaves from books, magazines and newspapers mixed with autumn leaves from the garden trees as if the latter could somehow sweeten the atrabilious smoke of the former.

The chanting of matins summoned her, yet under a greater obedience she was also burning her own obsession. She must. Otherwise how could she concentrate on the only matter of true consequence: salvation.

Amid the smoke names flared and burnt to black: Arnold, Holden, Morton, Dimbleby, Junor, Cohen, Brown, Whitelaw, Adams, Wilson, McGuinness. Blair and other names: Burrell, Windsor, Bowles, Hewitt, Hoare, Mannakee, Khan, Al Fayed, d'Estaing. D'Estaing? And more recognisable: Harrods, Mercedes, Fiat, Pakistan, France, Wales, Wills and Harry.

At a photograph torn from a magazine she paused to read her own scrawl: *HRH DS at Enniskillen War Memorial (Who 6/12/1993 Australian edition America's People). No mention of this event sighted in posthumous official inquiries/ reports. Outside terms of reference?*

Into the fire it went. And the smoke from it rose to drift across Ireland and the Irish Sea towards a lake island where lay interred Diana Spencer, sometime kindergarten teacher, sometime Her Royal Highness, The Princess of Wales, untimely dead, a mystery shrouded in a legend woven from the raw facts of the paper leaves.

The last of them were in her hands, a photocopied typescript inspired by the Enniskillen event. The nun riffled through the typescript leaves, recalling their arrival years before in an envelope, postmarked World's End, and addressed to: *Sister Mary of the Cross, c/o the Convent of the Good Shepherd, Co. Connemara, All Ireland.*

The covering note clipped to the typescript said: *Not suggesting that this may interest you under your religious name; it may, however, interest under your birth name or under your noms de guerre if only because of the haunting possibility that publication of this fiction when Diana Spencer was still alive might have altered the life-style that led to her death at Paris in 1997.*

Could fiction alter fact? She tore the typescript apart and dropped the leaves into the fire.

The last copy?

– 1 –

The Ritz Hotel, London, W.1

Home-marker thought Guthrie—Alisdair, Major, Scots Guards—and turned off Piccadilly into Green Park, his combat boots thudding on a tarmac path. Home. He smiled to himself. Across the park, Buckingham Palace floated in a mist, lit by the rising July sun, its leviathan bulk ethereal, a wondrous dwelling from a fairy-tale.

Fairy-tale: his mother's phrase when she heard of his appointment as an Extra Equerry to the Queen. 'It's like a fairy-tale come true.' A fairy-tale indeed. And during his mother's slow dying he had consoled her with facets of it.

Buckingham Palace itself: six hundred and sixty-one rooms or more. Three miles of corridors. Two thousand electric light bulbs. Three hundred clocks and synchronised with them as many retainers, including—a delight to his mother—the Yeoman of the Gold Plate, guardian of the treasure vault beneath the palace.

The Queen's bow-windowed study on the first floor overlooking the thirty-nine acres of garden and the lake with its ducks, swans, geese and flamingoes—flamingoes!—fed shrimp to maintain the pinkness of their plumage though never, he'd assured his mother, used for croquet, causing her to smile in remembrance of *Alice in Wonderland,* a favourite book.

The Closet, with its crimson damask wall coverings and crystal chandelier, where the Royal Family assembled before state receptions.

'And you pressed the spring, didn't you say, Alisdair?' his mother'd asked on the second telling. He had said, a white lie.

It'd been a bewigged, scarlet-coated footman who'd pressed the secret spring on the ebony cabinet which caused a section of the wall to swing open and allow the Royal Family to emerge into the White Drawing Room, all gilt and dove-grey with yellow upholstered chairs where the guest waited, awed by the legerdemain.

Beneath his camouflage battledress, Guthrie was sweating but not enough to purge the previous night's booze: port too often passed at his annual Brigade Squad re-union. He increased his pace.

On the palace's central flagstaff, the royal standard was broken out, its quarterings blood-red and azure carrying the lions passant, guardant of England, the lion rampant of Scotland and the harp of Ireland, golden all. On this day Guthrie knew the standard was not a diversion for potential terrorists. The Queen **was** in residence. By now, her calling tray would've been taken into her bedroom overlooking Constitution Hill.

Guthrie was glad he'd arranged to be off-duty. The Queen missed nothing, including an equerry's hang-over, and said nothing. Her eye, however, could chill in a way to make a man remember the scrutiny of a drill sergeant on morning parade discovering dirty flesh, a shaving cut.

A truck marked EIIR Royal Farms was parked at the north, side entrance to the palace. One guard was examining the underside of the truck's chassis with a mirror on a pole. The other was questioning the driver about his lateness.

The driver—fit, tanned—said: 'Had to change a frigging tyre, didn't I?' Matter-of-fact. Too matter-of-fact? Too fit? Too tanned? And he glanced at Guthrie who avoided eye-contact.

The mirror on the pole guard sketched a present arms to Guthrie. Cheeky sod. None cheekier. Not usually dozy.

Guthrie passed the closer inspection of a wall-mounted camera and a clerk whose hard look made a redoubt of his desk. The amber light on the double security doors controlled by the clerk changed to green.

He was inside the magic citadel, and hearing faint, potent and a bit a problem for him, bagpipe music: *The Crags of Tumbledown Mountain.* Pipe-Major Roy Morrison of his own regiment playing for the Queen. 'Going to work on piping-hot eggs Benedict' was a palace joke about the Queen's favourite breakfast and music.

Guthrie had a problem, most immediate. From beneath his camouflage top, he took a walkie-talkie and thumbed it on. 'Duty officer? Monitor at Entrance Delta. Call out your guard. Perimeter defence is under test by a couple of would-be Fagans from the Redhill Sports and Social Club.'

Fagans: intruders, derived from Michael Fagan who twice in 1982 penetrated the palace, the second time confronting the Queen in her bedroom who, cooler than cucumber, had a smoke with him.

Redhill Sports and Social Club: S.A.S., Special Air Service Regiment.

Guthrie stayed in position until he heard the thump of boots, the rattle of equipment and raised voices, the guard challenging the occupants of the truck.

The lift to the second floor was empty. As Guthrie made his way along the red carpeted corridor to his room, he was planning a hot bath. Pamela Fitzgibbon, lady clerk in palace lingo, not secretary, had a different plan. 'Yum. Heavenly. Sweat.'

She'd been waiting for him, eager, overwhelming his protest. 'No order of the bath for you, my bonny lad.' She was licking him. 'Yummyyum-yum. Honest sweat. In this place.' She was stripping him and licking him along the salty valley of his spine. 'Most noble order of the garter belt for you.' This, though evocative, was not accurate. She was naked and, having stripped him, had him astride her and was carrying him back—wildly back—to their first meeting: the staff Christmas party. Mess nights of outrageous conviviality, he had survived, the genteel, drunken rout of that party dumbfounded him: the royal family under a crystal blaze of chandeliers moving to slow music, like the sacred puppets of some strange cult amid the tipsy swirl of their retainers.

The Queen, eternal Girl Guide. Princess Margaret, young delight of a generation, now with the look of a Manchu dowager. Prince Philip as stiffly cheery as a ship's figurehead. Prince Charles, bumpkin-cheeked yet gigolo-smooth on the dance floor. Princess Diana, elegant, lightsome, yet with a flicker of uncertainty about her.

One moment Guthrie was gazing raptly at her, the next he was waltzing with a palace transvestite who, despite a ball gown of such pastel gorgeousness it could have been a hand-me-down from the Queen Mother, insisted on leading until Pamela Fitzgibbon cut in, candle-pale, red hair aflame.

Guthrie told her the party reminded him of Boxing Day with his regiment, and the officers serving the other ranks food and drink. A memory she capped, telling him the Boxing Day tradition was a remnant of Saturnalia, the Roman winter feast when slaves became masters and mistresses for a day in an atavistic urge to disorder.

'So why?' he'd said, 'isn't the Queen dressed as a maid and the maid dressed as the Queen.'

'Too many queens in the palace already.'

They'd laughed together for the first time. And laughter between a man and a woman can be as significant as an orgasm.

Which they were now approaching at a closing speed of such profound mutual impact that it left them sprawled in panting silence.

A silence he broke with a cliché. 'Penny for your thoughts.'

'I haven't got any. Not one, except ... She touched him. 'Marvellous.'

'Ach, all right.' His accent parodied that of men he'd commanded. 'Ah'll gi'e ye tuppence.'

She giggled. 'You know I don't take money from you.'

Their exchange was the prelude to the game everyone in the palace played, the game of gossip, all the more exciting for the knowledge that they spoke first of what millions waited to hear more or less distorted by traffickers in old leaks.

Elbow on pillow, head propped on hand, she waited for him to speak. When he did, it was not about his part in countering the S.A.S. test of palace security, his secret work. He spoke of something connected to his cover as equerry.

'There's a petition up to the Queen. Subject: the privilege of playing the bagpipes under her window. The Micks want to share it.'

'And you're to advise?'

'Sooner rather than later's the word. Complicated. I mean, it's not only the Queen, there's Bobo to consider.' Bobo: Margaret Macdonald, the Queen's Scot's nanny who still behaved as if the palace was an extension of her former domain, the nursery.

'Suggest a compromise, why don't you? The Micks to play their uileann pipes on St Patrick's Day.' *Uileann.* She was watching his reaction to the word. She needed to find out how clever he was, and was taking risks to find out.

'Brilliant,' he said. 'How was your death watch?' He meant her night duty in the palace press office.

'Not so brilliant. That office is the last part of the British Empire on which the sun never sets.'

'Rough?'

'The roughest. Australians, you get them slightly cockneyfied during the day from Fortress Wapping and then at night you get them totally cockneyfied from Sydney or wherever.' Her voice went nasal, whiney. 'Any truth in the story Prince Charlie's nickname in London is Coeur de Tampon—you know?—like Richard Coeur de Lion.'

He was listening more to her body, her heartbeat, her breathing, than to her voice. 'No truth in it, of course.'

'Not a breath. That vile tape, Sydney Smartarse esquire wanted to tease another line out of it by getting me to validate the phoney nickname with a denial. Blasted tape. And the Squidgy one. I wish I knew who released them. I'd …'

She touched Guthrie where it counted. 'Not guilty, your honour.' He kissed her. 'If that's what you're going to do, you'll have to catch some strange, very strange, gents by the balls, too. Not easy. Dodgy bastards, the lot of them.'

She kissed him. 'I'm not sure I care for bastard as a pejorative.'

'Ah, yes, the Norman-Irish Fitzes, bastards all, your ancestor, the greatest of them.'

Was he trying to get her into a change of story? If so, he might have been checking on her. 'John,' she said. 'First Earl of Clare. I'm not a direct descendant. Collateral only.'

'Indeed.' He had been checking. No problem. She had already been checked by MI5's anti-domestic terrorism F branch. 'Not a exactly a beloved bastard your ancestor,' Guthrie was saying. 'Postponed Catholic Emancipation, effected the parliamentary union between England and Ireland and had his funeral broken up by a mob.'

During this recital he'd been responding to her in other ways. 'Oh, God,' he said. Maybe, he meant, Oh, Goddess.

She in the telepathic half-trance that sex can induce, thought of a line of finishing school French: '*Venus tout entiere a sa proie attachée*'—Venus, all of her, to her prey attached. She was astride him now, her red hair falling about her like the foliage of some beguiling tree, her breasts its pear-like fruit, golden in the sunlight reflected off the room's brocade curtains, her eyes green, intent.

He pulled her towards him to gorge on her breasts. As if his life depended on her.

It did.

– 2 –

Calcutta. London. S.E.1

Garbo shifted on the layer of newspapers which formed his bed inside a refrigerator carton as rain pattered on the plastic sheeting that waterproofed it. Coughing, moaning and abrupt disjointed cries, some of pleasure, penetrated the carton's sides: Wankers Anonymous in session. Or maybe even couples seized by the urge to procreate in this carton hamlet the way they did in the original Calcutta, Kipling's 'city of dreadful night', now by an obscene twist of the raj, replicated in London. It was as if—shit, what a thought—Maggie Thatcher, that blonde, imperiously genteel barmaid of politics, had been possessed by an avatar mightier than monetarism: Kali, the Dark One, the bountiful, the destroyer, with a new kind of thugee and a remorseless band of practitioners.

Bugger 'em all, Garbo thought. Bugger 'em all. The long broker, the short speculator and the tall banker whose game was wasting people for money. Garbo spat a bullet of night phlegm against the carton wall. His game, too.

The wind carried to him the sound of Big Ben striking the hours.

Six.

06.00 hours.

Stand to.

He eased himself from the carton, already fully dressed in an old, black tracksuit, black joggers and a greasy trench-coat. He rubbed his whiskers as he checked his surroundings. The rain was easing off. In the early light, the circular wall enclosing the carton hamlet could've been that of an ancient hill-fort. Nearby two figures were wrestling. Or embracing. He tightened the rope round the trench-coat waist. The way from the hamlet was by dripping tunnels and slippery ramps, smelling of piss and shit. He added his quota-of both.

Like a dog marking its territory.

Or a tiger.

Except that his gait was the shuffle of a punchy boxer forever fated to rub his boot soles in the rosin tray of defeat.

From Waterloo tube station, he caught a train, amused at how even rough heads tended to avoid him. Might be an idea to market old clothes as security gear. Add some pissy-shitty aftershave and it would mean guaranteed protection for the rich.

Cheaper than a bullet-proof Roller.

Safer than a flak jacket.

At Gloucester Road station, he used the spiral stair not the lift, running up it with a silent speed at odds with his earlier punchy shuffle. This he resumed for his approach to the apartment of the subject: Warren Munro, 43, single, executive All Corporate Equities. One of a team of nine in the ACE London office who provided a 24-hour, seven days a week linkage with headquarters in Melbourne and outposts in Paris, Monte Carlo, Rome, Geneva, New York, Los Angeles and Hong Kong.

Garbo had been briefed on Munro's roster. Three-week cycle: 09.00—17.00, 17.00—01.00, 01.00—09.00. He had double-checked this, trailing Munro from his apartment to his office and back again, having in the past been involved in situations where unchecked briefings spelled total snafu.

Not easy, the tailing. Munro's office was in Bishopsgate where the Irish Republican Army had detonated a blockbuster at No. 99, which became the focus of a security cordon: road blocks, vehicle checks and uniformed police armed with more than truncheons and their traditional tough placidity. In addition there were roving plainclothes patrols of his own kind of specialist, nondescript except for their eyes.

Munro, a strict time-keeper, left his apartment one hour before his start time and returned to it within one hour of his finish time.

No drinks with the boys for Warren Munro.

Nor with the girls either.

Loner.

Loner who'd sniffed out too much for his own good? Poor bastard.

Positioned behind the low stone wall of a church garden, Garbo touched his trench-coat rope. Munro's apartment was opposite: ground floor of a three-storey terrace with basement. Black front door with security intercoms under a white portico reached by seven steps. Below the steps was the door to the basement. He had already weighed the pros and cons of which Munro shift best served the objective.

09.00—17.00.

Day infiltration.

Night ex-filtration.

From the pocket of his trench coat, he took a wristwatch: Omega Seamaster, digital, titanium, tantalum and gold.

Time: 07.59.

The front door opened. Warren Munro appeared: height, five-ten, weight 160 pounds, tanned, fit, but fit for what? Dapper in a dark city suit and carrying a black briefcase decorated with a green and red Gucci riband. As he reached the bottom step, he looked back at his apartment.

Checking to make sure he hasn't left a window open, Garbo thought.

Munro turned into Courtfield Gardens, its left-hand pavement narrow. He crossed to the right while Garbo kept to the left, past the railed garden square onto which the terrace backed.

Beaut!

The sun was breaking through. In the garden, a jaunty cove—silver hair, silver moustache, bright plaid shirt, brown corduroys, green wellies—was moving proprietorially. Garbo's briefing had included the occupants of the apartments. The cove was Ralph Bowman, ex-R.A.F. wireless operator/air gunner. Clearly he relished his role: Squire of Basement Hall.

Munro had increased his lead and was passing a red brick terrace marked with a blue plaque commemorating the actress Ellen Terry. Garbo quickened his pace and was right behind Munro at Earls Court Station. There, Garbo saw Munro onto his usual train to the City.

He did not follow him. Instead he cut down Earls Court Road to Old Brompton Road. From a flower shop—Victoria Flora—he bought a basket of red and yellow roses mixed with maidenhair fern.

The assistant's sniffy distaste for his appearance was mollified by the crispness of his money. He looked helpless when she said, 'Do you want to write a card?' He nodded when she said, 'What if I write it?'

'Love,' he said. 'Just write love.'

She did and put the card among the roses.

He took the basket. 'For Mum.'

In the midst of duplicity, a leaven of truth.

The assistant watched him shuffle in the direction of Brompton Cemetery. Not that he was bound there. He turned into Warwick Road and his forward base: a rented bed-sitter, possibly pioneered in the Sixties by a fellow Australian; it had a small shower alcove installed in the kitchen area.

He stripped off and showered, shaving by touch under the shower, before drying himself. He broke two eggs into a yellow plastic bowl, beat them with a fork and dipped four slices of white bread in the egg mixture which he fried in bacon fat while he dressed: khaki shirt, cotton drill trousers and desert boots: a semblance of uniform which pleased him.

The bread he turned to fry its other side and made a pot of tea. He wolfed down the French toast with two cups of tea. Black. Three sugars for an energy kick. He washed the dishes, cutlery and frying pan and emptied the teapot.

Nothing worse than a shit-order base-camp.

His trousers were already belted. Over the belt, he wrapped the rope from his trench coat, making sure it was covered by the white windbreaker that completed his rig.

The basket of red and yellow roses waited, fresh as a child's morning.

Time: 09.20.

– 3 –

Buckingham Palace. London, S.W.1

D'Acre—Rex, courtier—gazed at the mandarin group in one of the Chinese Dining Room's wall-hangings. Most visitors dismissed the hangings as gaudy relics from that magnificent folly: the Royal Pavilion, Brighton, seven years a-building by John Nash for George Augustus Frederick of Hanover, Prince Regent during the mad spells of his father George III, who mislaid the American colonies.

Moving round the room, inspecting its ornate gilded furniture, D'Acre mused. The Prince Regent might've been less inspired by extravagant taste than by nostalgia for the immemorial stability of imperial China.

Certainly, beneath his foppish exterior, he was dissolute and ruthless enough for any of the Forbidden City's emperors. His first and secret wife, the Catholic Maria Anne Fitzherbert he'd rejected when this became a condition of his Government's paying his debts.

His subsequent dynastic marriage to Caroline of Brunswick he'd ended no less ruthlessly after a year and a daughter, the pair separating to beget gossip about their respective indiscretions. Hers so spectacular that he instigated the 'Delicate Investigation' of 1805.

She responded with a book—The Book—secretly printed. No serial rights for her, however. It was swiftly suppressed before she went cavorting in Europe, bold as gold and twice as popular, bawdy, topless, begetting another commission in 1818, two years before the death of

George III opened for her the prospect of being Queen Consort—or, 'by God, she would blow the King off his throne'.

As she might've with the revelation that the secret Fitzherbert marriage had been validated by the Pope.

Heyday for early press hounds.

The rakehell ruler of a rakehell era having a Bill of Pains and Penalties introduced in the House of Lords to dissolve Caroline's marriage and privileges. The Bill lapsing, she, under the influence of, 'nervous medicines and laudanum', trying to enter Westminster Abbey for her husband's coronation only to-be prevented, and dying a year later.

'That Bedlam Bitch of a Queen', according to Sir Walter Scott.

D'Acre paused before the ormolu and blue enamel clock on the room's gilt and white marble fireplace.

Only one year.

And an undiagnosed illness.

Opportune enough for George IV to enjoy nine years of rule: the *sine qua non* of happy monarchs—and happy courtiers—uninterrupted tenure. Nonetheless, princes could be personally ruthless in those days. They were part of the natural order. As for doubting scribes, they soon got their comeuppance; even the founder of *The Times,* John Walter was not immune: banged up in Newgate for alleging Prince George and his siblings were less than overjoyed when their papa, the King, recovered from his bouts of insanity.

Sixteen months gaol. Plus one hour in the Charing Cross pillory.

D'Acre sat down in a faded pink upholstered chair before the room's rosewood dining table. Scribes. He loathed their self-serving whining about press freedom. Prostitutes, all of them: bought and sold with their brothels by the likes of mad Northcliffe, sly Beaverbrook, sleazy

Hearst, sanctimonious Luce, artful Murdoch, verbose Black and the Genghis Khan of them all, Robert Maxwell.

Rising, D'Acre could see his reflection in the gilt-pillared mirror above the fireplace. Elegant. Austere. Holbein, he liked to think, not Van Dyck; Tudor not Stuart.

The knock on the dining-room door was tentative. D'Acre turned from the mirror as a footman emerged from behind the red folding screen that covered the doorway. Young. Dark. Handsome, suavity not yet overlaying his natural eagerness. 'Oh, it's you, Mr. D'Acre. Sorry, sir, there's a lunch.'

'Luncheon? Why of course. Marcus, isn't it? Her Majesty and five guests, including Canterbury.'

Marcus, impressed by D'Acre's knowing the Queen was having the Archbishop of Canterbury to lunch, said. 'Yes, sir.'

Not only deference but the intonations of deference were minutely important here. Outside the dining room, D'Acre wondered whether there hadn't been a fresh depth of deference in the footman's tone.

The Palace grapevine worked with incredible speed. Already the footman might well know that His Royal Highness Prince Charles and Her Royal Highness the Princess Diana were seeking Rex D'Acre for their respective households.

– 4 –

Earl's Court, London, S.W.5

Garbo passed the garden square again at 09.45. Ralph Bowman, the Squire of Basement Hall, was astride a ride-on mower cutting the garden lawn.

One minute later, Garbo was beside the front door of the Munro terrace. From the pocket of his windbreaker, he took a white baseball cap and put it on, pulling the brim low. Better than dark glasses, less hostile.

He pressed the intercom button for the third-floor apartment. A woman's voice answered impatiently, as if interrupted.

'Yes, who is it?'

'Flowers for Ms. Meldrum.'

'Flowers?'

'That is Ms. Sally Meldrum, isn't it?'

'Yes ... but—.'

'Look, love. I've got other deliveries if you don't mind.'

The intercom buzzed and the black door clicked open.

Facing Garbo was an old-fashioned cage lift. To his left was the door of Munro's apartment. The lift groaned upwards. Sally Meldrum was waiting, framed in her doorway. Tall. Dark cap of hair. Blue, paint-spotted shirt. Blue jeans. Blue eyes, gazing at Garbo appraisingly. She took the basket of flowers and read the card. 'You wouldn't happen to know who sent them?' She proffered a coin. Garbo took it. 'Ta, love. Na, I only deliver.'

She was already turning away, smiling as if a possible answer had occurred to her. Garbo, getting back into the lift, wondered which lucky bugger might be going to benefit from the flowers. If Ms Sally Meldrum did ring the flower-card number, she would be left with a double puzzle: the identity of the old tramp who'd ordered red and yellow roses and the identity of the fit young guy who'd delivered them.

On the ground floor, Garbo opened the front door, slammed it and pulling on a pair of gloves turned for Munro's.

Deadlock.

Plastic strip no good.

Picklock. He was inside the flat in 90 seconds, breathing its silence taking in its curtain-drawn gloom, his heartbeat measured. And quickening in an adrenalin spurt as his briefing, and his double check, blew up in his face:

'Warren?'

Woman's voice.

Mother?

Sister?

Sweetheart?

Sweetheart. For sure. Sudden sweetheart, framed in the bedroom doorway, saying, 'Carissimo', and moved in a golden shimmer of nightdress across the polished wood floor.

Hesitating—a dancer realising her *pas de deux* could be fatal—her eyes widening, photographing her partner for the mug-shots of hell.

Anger supercharged Garbo's adrenalin rush. He moved swiftly to cut her off her retreat to the bedroom. She glided sideways, graceful even in fear, making for the bathroom, her long, fair ponytail streaming behind her.

He pivoted. She was at the bathroom doorway when he reached out and grabbed her hair to pull her back towards him. Her hair—a false switch—came away in his hand. And she was through the doorway, her screams, an aria of terror, beginning to ricochet off the bathroom tiles as she clicked the door-bolt home. The click gave him his aiming point: once, twice, he booted the door with the flat of his foot. The door splintered and he shouldered it open.

She had armed herself and stopped screaming to jab at him with her weapon.

A toothbrush.

Electric.

Ridiculous.

No more than his throwing her hairpiece to blind her for a moment, as his hands went out to blind her forever.

Carotid pressure. Minimum bruising.

All the while listening not only to her dying gasps but for the sound of inquiring voices, footsteps, the bell rung or the door knocked by someone who'd heard her scream.

Nothing.

His instinct was to scrub and withdraw. Not on. He had a deadline for the elimination of Warren Munro.

Today.

No way could he cut and come again. He stood up from the low white chair where he'd sat after eliminating her—a possible alternative scenario forming. He bent down and closed her hard-staring eyes.

Sweetheart.

Munro—Carissimo—would've done no less. Garbo became Munro as he stripped off her nightdress. It was wet. Fear-piss. Could've been worse. He laid her in the bath, put the plug in and turned on the taps, adjusting them to get a tepid mix, and adding a generous splash of bubble-bath liquid which foamed from the impact of the running water.

He watched the white foam creep over her tanned body and turned off the taps when the foam covered her pale breasts. Some of the water he scooped up and splashed over the nightdress. It would conceal the other wetness. And the tepid water would fudge the time of her death. Her hands and forearms he laid along the sides of the bath. Must avoid the washer-woman effect.

Wrinkled hands.

Dead giveaway.

Sweetheart must've come to the apartment after he'd ceased surveillance, certain Munro was spending another solitary night at home.

No loner Munro.

He'd been saving himself up for Sweetheart. As who wouldn't? Left her in bed sated yet still eager enough to think he'd returned early to her irresistible presence.

Warren? ... Carissimo ...

Garbo left the bathroom. No, Sweetheart, not Carissimo—your friendly local double tapper.

He'd been briefed on the lay-out of the apartment. Not its luxury. The main bedroom contained a cherry-wood sleigh bed, its white linen sheets and silk-covered duvet rumpled and twisted from sexual tussle. On a cherry-wood dressing table was a green leather make-up case.

Off the bedroom was a dressing-room: suits, seven, dinner jackets, two, Burberry, one and wire-stack baskets of shirts, ties, jerseys, socks and gloves above a parade of shoes and boots—ski and rugby. Racquets—tennis, squash. And a surfboard. *Duke Kahanamoku's Own.* Great surfer. Greater swimmer: Hundred metres Olympic gold,

1912, 1920, second to Johnny Weissmuller, 1924.

Two matching suitcases of green leather stood inside the dressing room, one opened. Sweetheart must've paused only long enough to take off her make-up and put on her night togs. He examined the luggage tags: Donella Ricci—Roma. Lucky Munro. Exogamist. No tight-lipped, gidgee-tough Aussie sheilas for him.

The long living-room was furnished club-style, its floor islanded with Turkish rugs. On either side of a baronial red brick fireplace was a button-backed maroon-leather couch. The dark, panelled walls were decorated with a set of Ronald Searle prints about various old-time cures.

> ***For The Toothache 17th Century***
> *Go between the sun and the sky to a ford,*
> *a place where the dead and the living cross,*
> *lift a stone from it (the ford) with the teeth,*
> *and the toothache vanishes.*

No cure for death. In the corner by the fireplace was a heavily freighted drinks trolley: gin, rum, brandy, sherry, vodka—Polish and Russian—various whiskies—Scotch, Irish, Canadian, Japanese and Bourbon. He needed a drink. In the kitchen, copper saucepans gleamed on a rail above a central scrubbed butcher's block. At a double gas stove, he made himself a cup of instant Nescafé. Black. Three sugars.

Garbo thought of himself as an actor. By a system of nil-personal contact the agent who retained him had reinforced his rule not to wonder about the background of subjects nor the whys and wherefores of their elimination. Sudden Sweetheart's elimination had been forced. Swallowing the coffee and surveying the kitchen, he broke his rule.

Obviously something of a gourmet: Munro. Up for elimination for cooking the books on his own behalf?

Possible.

The briefing on Munro had come from an insider. This flash apartment was that of another insider. Munro's London posting meant he knew how many beans made five for the investors and for the other insiders. All Corporate Equities had to be one of those cowboy operations where the insiders wore neither black hats nor white. Grey was their go: big, grey ten-gallon hats to hide the loot in.

No shortage of loot either—cowboys riding off in all directions—after the deregulation of the Australian financial system at the urging of economists who'd picked up monetarist nostrums from Maggie Kali's votaries and passed them to a Mick Labor—Labor!—minister who'd treated them like the eternal verities he'd learned from his childhood teachers.

Had Munro found out about some humungous scam—phantom trades, profit diversion, money laundering—and demanded more beans? Plus more perks. Bigger apartment. Maybe a car—Jag, Roller, Merc—with chauffeur to impress Sweetheart but not to do the chauffeur thing: boff the boss's squeeze.

Humungous scam. Yeah, maybe. But suppose Munro didn't want in? What if he wanted out because he knew the posse was riding the ranges rounding up the baddies and he didn't fancy jail?

Munro could've told someone he was going to negotiate an indemnity deal and blow the whistle. Someone he trusted. Sweetheart? She …

Garbo looked into his cup. Tea, he should've had tea. Reading the tea-leaves would've made more sense than speculation which at the end of the day—this day—would not matter.

Never did.

He finished the coffee and washed and dried the cup before replacing it.

Time: 11.20.

In the bathroom he added more water to the bath without looking at Sweetheart's body. His training was to harbour up and rest while waiting for action. He went to the double bed. And had a weird twinge. What if Munro had made Sweetheart pregnant? A decisive twinge.

It made him resolve never to speculate on a subject again. There was a second bedroom with a single bed overlooking the garden square. Ralph Bowman, the Squire of Basement Hall, was spreading the lawn clippings as mulch beneath the garden's rhododendrons.

Garbo returned to the living room and lay down on one of the couches after setting his watch alarm for 17.00 hours, giving him an hour to prepare for Munro. To sleep, he lay on the floor, off to the side of the apartment's front door.

– 5 –

Buckingham Palace, London, S.W.1

Motes of history drifted in the sunlit gallery where Edward VII had taken his cane to vandalise busts of his mother Queen Victoria's 'constant personal attendant', the bibulous John Brown who twice risked his life to save hers.

Downstairs in Marble Hall, D'Acre let one thought fill his mind: anticipation is the secret of preferment.

In the sumptuous rooms of the Belgian Suite with their garden views, he was less interested in the Zoffany portraits of George III and Queen Charlotte than in Gainsborough's *Diana and Actaeon.*

He could not be the only person to appreciate the irony of that painting there and then: Actaeon who had viewed Diana naked, turned by her into a stag, torn to pieces by his own hounds.

The creep-hounds of Fleet now kenneled in Wapping, Kensington and Canary Wharf.

Prince Charles they'd hunted since he sipped a schoolboy cherry brandy. He was inured to them. Not so the Princess Diana, harried since her legs were first seen sunlit through her skirt. So fair a princess yet so frail, daughter of a bolter mother and a belted—some said belting—earl. She should not have to endure such harassment even if she seemed, poor child, to seek it.

In his office, situated off the Privy Purse Corridor, D'Acre concentrated on his specific duty: keeping the master log of royal events, collating data from the offices of the Queen and Prince Philip's private secretaries in the Palace itself with data from Prince Charles' secretary in St James Palace and that of Princess Diana's secretary in Kensington Palace, the Queen Mother's secretary in Clarence House as well as the secretaries of Princess Anne, Prince Andrew, Prince Edward and lesser royals.

His duty: to ensure that no headline-inducing duplications or meetings took place in the months ahead, particularly between Prince Charles and Princess Diana. He paused in his work. Perhaps he should open a line of communication on Camilla Parker-Bowles. There surely lay the crux of embarrassment. If only it were possible to replicate the style of Edward VII. No wonder the French admired him.

He knew how close to farce his ancestor George IV had sailed. Even closer, the cock-a-leg sea-dog William IV with Dorothy Jordan, his actress mistress of twenty years and ten bastards. He knew farce can be as destructive to dynasty as tragedy. He'd simply refused to let La Camilla's great-grandma and his mistress, Alice Keppel, become a problem vis-à-vis his Queen Consort, Alexandra.

Oh, lucky master of style to have his royal consort invite his commoner mistress to join her in a duet at his deathbed. Masters less lucky, less stylish with wives more intractable, more self-destructive needed help to solve their potentially disastrous problems.

Anticipatory help.

D'Acre was checking cross-referenced columns of dates for royal events, one, two, three, four months ahead in 1993. No hackable computer file for him. Everything in the master-log, he was pleased to hear was known as, 'D'Acre's Domesday Book', handwritten in modified Gothic chancellery cursive with one of his collection of fountain pens: Mont Blanc, Parker, Schaeffer and the great Waterman trio, the Pickwick, the Owl and the Waverley. He was using the latter and stopped at November.

Eleventh month. Eleventh day. Eleventh hour. Thursday. Remembrance Day.

And the following Sunday, the fourteenth, the fifteenth being HRH Prince Charles' birthday.

How things had changed since the formal separation announcement on December 9, 1992.

Prince Charles and his wife, the Princess Diana were not listed to attend the national commemoration service at the Cenotaph in Whitehall together. They were attending different events.

D'Acre bit the end of his pen. The Prince's he could understand. The Princess's? Surely not? A mistake—gross—household staffs distracted under the barrage and counter-barrage of media coverage.

As he reached for his telephone to double-check, D'Acre's eye was caught by a silver-framed photograph on his desk, showing Prince Charles and Princess Diana, one of many taken by press photographers throughout the world. In this one, he was caught between them. He was convinced the photograph had led to his being singled out for advancement.

And ultimate responsibility.

– 6 –

Earl's Court, London, S.W.5

Garbo awakened. Not his Seamaster alarm: Warren Munro's opening the apartment door and saying: 'Guess who took an early mark.'

Early mark. Boy home from school. Eager. But not for books.

In one silent movement, Garbo came off the floor, the open door concealing him. In another single movement, he unwound the rope from his waist even as Munro was closing the door and starting for the bedroom.

'You there, D—?''

Donella? Dear? Darling?

The rope round his neck cut off his last endearment. And Garbo's crossed hands were tightening the loop as his left knee went into Munro's back for leverage.

Munro's hands clawed at the rope.

Mug, Garbo thought. If your numbered marble had come up in the Aussie Vietnam lottery like mine, you might've learned a counter move or two.

Elbow strike.

Shin kick.

Leg behind the attacker's leg, going backwards with him to break the pressure.

Munro kept fighting the rope, his own strength increasing its lethal effect. The designation of the course, Garbo took, was Silent Killing. A misnomer, he always thought. No one died silently any more than they were born silently. Munro struggled like a rabbit strangling itself in a snare. Big buck rabbit. Big grunts. Big groans. Big gurgles. Big silence.

Poor bloody bunny.

Garbo rolled the body onto a rug and pulled the rug over the polished floor to the bathroom.

There he made a running noose in the rope and put the noose round Munro's neck. He propped Munro's body upright on the low chair in the bathroom and threw the free end of the rope over the top of the bathroom door, securing it to the door handle.

The low chair he kicked free of Munro's feet, toppling it over. Munro's feet almost touched the floor. And the swing of the door meant that he was gazing in final agony at Sweetheart in the bath.

Perfect.

Even the splintered catch worked for the scenario.

Lovers quarrel.

Sweetheart decides to take a bath.

Munro kicks door in.

Strangles Sweetheart in her bath.

Hangs himself in remorse.

Absolutely perfect.

Garbo rubbed his hands.

His gloved hands.

Not quite absolutely perfect.

For a split, nervy second, he was in a quandary.

Put his gloves on Munro's dead hands?

Create a match for the marks on Sweetheart's neck?

The dressing room.

He took a pair of Munro's own gloves, tan pigskin.

And eased them onto Munro's dead hands.

But only after he'd wetted the gloves with bathwater as he turned on the water taps.

The rug he'd used to transport the body, he replaced. No scuff marks.

As he left, his windbreaker reversed from white to brown, the lift groaned: an uncanny echo of Warren Munro's last sound.

From the row of telephones near Earls Court post office, he made a telephone call. There was no human response. He spoke to the hissing silence of a voice-activated tape-recorder.

'Our Aussie surfing friend got himself dumped by the wave he was on. Not a breath left in him. Oh, his sweetheart turned up. You didn't tell me about her, did you? Way it now looks they may have had a bit of a quarrel and decided that a final trip together was the only solution. You owe me for her. Standard fee.'

He hung up.

Time: 18.15.

Another hour he estimated, before the trickle of water into Sweetheart's bath caused it to overflow and Ralph Bowman, the Squire of Basement Hall, to start knocking on doors and raising the alarm.

Along Earls Court Road, the evening tide of traffic fumed and growled as it flowed to various destinations and a single notion.

Get-away.

– 7 –

Buckingham Palace, London. S.W.1

Guthrie entered the Household Dining Room from the 1855 Room with its full-length portrait of the Emperor Napoleon III and the Empress Eugenie. A mistake. The voluptuous beauty of the empress was over-laid by the memory of the avid Pamela Fitzgibbon. As in a dream, he heard the tinkling of the silver bell with which the Master of the Household controlled the dining room's servants. He was brought back to the reality of the room: its lime-green walls, golden frieze, matching Indian carpet and intense conversation, the intensity deriving from the assurance of a select group. And there were fewer more select groups than the Royal Household.

Too select, Guthrie thought. Lady clerks such as Pamela Fitzgibbon were relegated to what some called the 'Naff Off Canteen', lowest of the eating rooms in the intricate upstairs-downstairs palace catering system.

Grandees for the use of, the Household Dining Room: the Lord Chamberlain, the Queen's Private Secretary, the members of the Honourable Corps of Gentlemen at Arms, the Keeper of the Privy Purse, the Crown Equerry, the Mistress of the Robes, the Ladies in Waiting. Guthrie himself tended to feel imposterish there and admired the aplomb with which Rex D'Acre was hobnobbing with the Lord Chamberlain and the Queen's Private Secretary.

Ubiquitous, indispensable Rex D'Acre, was Guthrie's appreciation.

One of those people whose peculiar genius it was to transcend the hierarchies of any given system. In his regiment, Guthrie had seen D'Acre's equivalent: the orderly room clerk who swung more influence than his rank indicated.

Guthrie took his place and ate celery soup, ordinary silver spoon not a rounded soup spoon, white bait, no fish knife, fish knives like soup spoons having been banned by Queen Victoria as evidence of 'modern vulgarity'. He followed the fish fish with grouse, which had the grit of fresh lead shot in it, and cheese: double Gloucester.

He ate as he might've eaten ration-pack scran in a battle zone, and the gambits of Lieutenant Commander Neville Lytton, a fellow equerry, made him wish he were in one. Of Lytton, Pamela Fitzgibbon had remarked: 'Heart of oak, no. Head of oak, yes.' Which made Guthrie think again of her supple avidity while he gazed out through the French windows over the balustraded terrace to the garden beyond.

'I say,' Lytton was saying. 'You didn't really recommend that the plod outside Her Majesty's bedroom should wear boots instead of the traditional carpet slippers?'

Guthrie admitted he had.

'Super,' Lytton said. 'Your remark that carpet slippers were all very well for Lord Lovat on D-Day but that he did carry a Tommy-gun.'

Omniscient as well as ubiquitous and indispensable: Rex D'Acre. Guthrie had only one glass of hock and one glass of claret. But D'Acre said: 'A turn in the garden to walk off your wine, my dear fellow, before we return to our loose-boxes.'

My dear fellow. As a Scot, Guthrie retained an aversion to such cold English endearments. Nevertheless, he accompanied D'Acre through the French windows onto the terrace and down its steps to the garden, mildly amused at D'Acre's follow-up remark: 'You seem to be settling in admirably.'

Settling in. Guthrie had been on Palace duty for two years. D'Acre was saying: 'Your ruffian alert the other morning has won you golden opinions.' Guthrie went into evasive incomprehension. 'Come now,' D'Acre said. 'I don't have to tell you the Purple One was mightily impressed not only by you personally but by the Coates Mission's choice of you.'

Guthrie in turn was impressed by D'Acre's use of Purple One, the security code name for the Queen and by his reference to the Coates Mission, the 'discreet elite' from the Household Division charged with protecting the Royal Family. D'Acre went on: 'I may tell you that the objective of the exercise was to carry off Purple One's personal piper.'

This was already known to Guthrie. His reaction had been pity for anyone—S.A.S. or not—trying to carry off Pipe Major Roy Morrison, a gentle-seeming bear of a Highlander, capable of berserker rage when physically challenged.

'I didn't realise our friends had a Charlie G with them.' Guthrie said. He meant a Carl Gustav 84-millimetre recoilless anti-tank weapon.

'Ha', D'Acre said. Whether this was a reaction to the witticism or to the beauty of the garden, Guthrie didn't know. 'Apropos piper,' D'Acre said. 'You can be assured your suggested compromise to enable Irish pipers to play under the Queen's window on St Patrick's Day is receiving serious consideration at the highest level.'

Guthrie was tempted to tell D'Acre the suggestion had come from Pamela Fitzgibbon. He did not. There was something off-putting as well as compelling about D'Acre's icy languor which Guthrie knew had made him a fortune back in the days when Lloyds spelt wealth.

English, D'Acre: mask on mask, an eternal courtier going back from pinstripe to knee breeches to doublet and hose and always with a dagger beneath his cloak. 'It's really too much,' he was saying. 'I can remember when the Scribes and Pharisees were clothed in Marks and Spencer raiment and preserved a decent decorum. Now they're into Turnbull and Asser and totally without shame. The Scribes write whatever takes their vulgar fancy. As for the Pharisees, even their slang is vile. They talk of blitzing Her Royal Highness, the Princess Diana, hosing her down, whacking her.'

'Fools,' Guthrie said.

'Fools,' D'Acre said, 'do have their place. "Alas, poor Yorick, I knew him well, a fellow of infinite jest … 'But the jest of these fellows is not merely infinitely tedious, it can be insufferably pompous. Yes, pompous. Someone was recalling at luncheon the famous—or possibly infamous—occasion when Her Majesty received a hoot of chief jesters alias editors. It was when the Princess of Wales was with child and had her picture taken while buying herself wine gums.'

'Rowntrees?'

Puzzlement fought disdain on D'Acre's face. Disdain won. 'That I don't know. What I do know is that one of the jesters had the effrontery to suggest to H.M., that if the Princess of Wales—"Lady Di" in his oik-speak—didn't want to have her picture taken she should send a footman for the wine gums.'

'And?'

'Devastation. Utter devastation. Her Majesty smiled as only she can—lethal radiance—and said: "What an extremely pompous man you are".'

'Obviously furious.'

'Should she have occasion to be furious? The jesters need to be taught their place. There are those of us who thought a prime opportunity was lost when the admirable Rupert Murdoch's *Sun* acquired the Queen's Christmas speech, and printed it in advance. An action for breach of copyright—say forty to fifty million—would have knocked Murdoch from the high wire where he was already tottering.'

'Rich as Croesus. I thought.'

'Only if golden touch covers other people's money. Murdoch is known to a multitude of banks. In his critical period, ten million—ten million dollars—could have knocked him off the high wire: the amount owed to an obscure Pittsburgh bank. Had that bank followed through on its decision to call in the loan, every other banker would've have been after him. Oh, what a feast! Oh what a fall for Humpty Dumpty Murdoch! And this king's man would not have tried to put him together again.'

'Could anyone?'

'Exactly. It is with that in mind that some of us are urging a number of strategic investments.'

'In newspapers?'

'Too obvious, much too obvious—though it might have been fun to read the rumours about who cuckolded Rupert Baretits and how he wooed and won his second honey. What we're discussing are strategic holdings in certain banks to which certain newspaper proprietors are beholden. You follow?'

Guthrie thought he did. He recalled newspaper coverage of events of the previous year: 1992, the Queen's *annus horribilis* which Paddy Sikorsky at the Brigade Squad re-union had translated as the, 'arsehole of a year'.

Rough yet apt: the marriage break-ups of Prince Charles and Princess Diana and of Prince Andrew and his Duchess, Sarah. The antique love-life of Prince Philip. The Queen's untaxed wealth. The great fire at Windsor Castle. Squidgygate and Camillagate.

'Squidgy,' Guthrie said. 'Fred and Gladys. Fergie and Randy Andy. The jesters aren't exactly making jokes without straw.'

D'Acre and Guthrie were walking by a lake where mallards set up a warning quacking against the dragon growl of traffic beyond the walls.

'Agreed,' D'Acre said. '"What light through yonder window breaks? It is the east and Squidgy is the sun!" isn't quite Shakespeare.'

'Or even the poet McGonagall.'

'Ha. The nicknames are ridiculous, almost as ridiculous as their behaviour. Always have been: Florizel and Perdita, the Prince Regent and the original Mrs. Robinson; Gussy and Goosy, the Prince Regent's brother Augustus and the Lady Augusta Murray; or Suss, his other nickname, in relation to his other inamorata Lady Cecilia Buggin alias Ciss? Ridiculous without doubt. The Crown itself, however, must not be made to appear ridiculous and should the behaviour of any person make it seem so ...'

'Send a few knighthoods in with the rations?'

'Not nowadays. Knighthoods, or benighthoods, are perceived as No. 10 rewards, not palace awards, except, of course, knighthoods of the Royal Victorian Order which are in the monarch's own gift. The others—wouldn't you say?—are devalued, grossly devalued. The rogues, vagabonds and privy-haunting martlets of the theatre were bad enough, the moons are beyond a joke.'

'Moons?'

'Television personalities whose passing celebrity merely reflects the fame of their interviewees.'

'And the moons, those who interview them, what're they called?'

'Loons, I suppose. Seriously what some of us have been recalling is how the House of Hanover dealt with its Scribes: gaol and the stocks. A return to such summary retribution is what is needed.'

'Rotten vegetables supplied by Fortnums?'

'You wouldn't know of anyone interested in meting out this retribution?'

'A battalion.' Guthrie was only half joking. 'But it will cost a fortune in McEwan's Export Ale.'

'Ha.' D'Acre said. 'We're not thinking of your regiment or indeed any of the foot guards. What we need is a ruffian, a funny, ready to chastise a sampling of the sub-species Scribe and Pharisee *pour encourager les autres.'*

Guthrie hesitated. D'Acre did not. He made the masonic sign of distress: his left arm rigid at his side, his head craned round over his right shoulder and his right hand shading his eyes.

Midway between amusement at this melodrama and embarrassment that he had once participated in it, Guthrie said: 'Don't worry. I may be able to help.'

Rain began to fall. They turned back on the gravel path. As they did, a small figure in a green herringbone coat followed by a trio of corgis and a footman in a scarlet coat, bearing a silver tray, emerged from the palace.

The ubiquitous, indispensable, omniscient Rex D'Acre recognised the corgis. 'Spark. Fable. Myth.'

Rain or no rain, Elizabeth the Second, Queen of the United Kingdom of Great Britain and Northern Ireland was going to feed her ducks, swans and flamingoes.

A small figure. Even forlorn. A forlorn hope. To Guthrie a student of his métier, this was no empty phrase but a technical term: a detachment appointed to lead in a service attended with uncommon peril.

He glanced up to where the Hilton Hotel loomed tall through the rain. Should never have been built: a classic sniper position. D'Acre had timing. 'Think of it,' he said, 'as a command performance from the Royal Patroness of Grand Lodge.'

– 8 –

Paradise, Glasgow. G40 3RE

Kern—Malkie, tool specialist—was watching the dying minutes of a Celtic-Rangers football match. He himself might have been dying so agonised was his body language in response to every pass.

A player in green and white got possession of the ball, advanced and hesitated as the blue-clad Rangers defenders covered his nearest team-mates. 'Would you look at him?' Kern said. 'Look, standing there like a superannuated ostrich, one foot on its egg, the other in the grave.' Move! he yelled, his voice breaking over the chant, 'Cel-tic! Cel-tic! Celtic!' like a seabird's over roaring waves. 'Move, you dopey git!'

The player did move, beating his man on the inside. 'Yes.' Kern yelled. And: 'In the name of the wee man,' as the player lost possession in the next tackle and the referee's whistle shrilled to end the match: Celtic 0, Rangers 0.

'To think a French reporter called the Celts, "L'orage" during their European Cup run,' Kern said. 'Some storm. Suffering from paralysis of the galluses, everyone of them.'

'Next time,' Garbo said. The game had been only vaguely comprehensible. His football was Australian Rules. His team, long ago and far-away, Port Adelaide. He had endured Kern's game because he knew that in Kern's other game as in his own, it was necessary while sizing up a prospect and his requirements to go through the motions of the ordinary.

Which they were continuing to do amid the bustling, arguing avalanche of supporters who released from the confines of Paradise—fond nickname for Celtic Stadium—spilled off the pavements into the roadway.

Behind them, a car hooted. Garbo moved to one side as did Kern. So did a stocky guy in a blue windcheater embellished with a blue and white scarf. After the car passed him, the guy kicked its offside rear-light, shattering it. The car braked and the passenger door opened. The stocky guy moved—not in retreat. He made the driver's side at a run, reached in with both hands and hauled the driver—not a small man—half-out of the car, simultaneously head-butting him.

By then the passenger had been joined by the two rear-seat occupants. They made a giant trio but the stocky guy turned to meet them as if they were midgets and he was King Kong.

'Cops.' Now Kern was moving—not to assist the law. Garbo got a wristlock on. him. 'No trouble. I want no trouble.' Kern struggled unavailingly. 'Look at them.'

The three big cops were jamming the stocky guy into the rear of the car. They didn't appear to be worrying about dents to its bodywork, or to the stocky guy's skull.

'Guess who's going to be sat on all the way to the nick?' Kern didn't wait for an answer. 'We should've steamed in the help the poor guy.'

Garbo was amused at the sympathy from Kern who was bald but not benign, his mug weathered, his nose rearranged. Not by a cosmetic surgeon. Garbo's amusement showed. Kern said: 'Here, you're never thinking I'm a Celtic supporter, are you? Or Rangers? Thistle. Thistle.' And noting Garbo's bewilderment, made it worse. 'Partick Thistle. Only went to the game to see how the opposition wis doin'.

Kern's van was painted battleship grey. Maybe to match the sky. Or his mood. 'Listen, pal. I've been thinking. No hard feelings an' a' the rest of it ...' His gaze had an edge, an edge Garbo had noticed in men wherever he went in this city. It was the gaze of an axeman calculating how a tall tree would fall if he struck it. 'Know what I mean?'

Garbo did. Malkie Kern's reputation although small was vivid, given the exclusive nature of his work, its outer limits set by ads in *Soldier of Fortune* magazine, its core deniable state-security operations. He was known for doing only what he wanted when he wanted and for whom he wanted. Garbo said: 'I thought we had a firm agreement.'

'Aye, we did, a firm agreement I'd give your requirements serious consideration. Well, I have. An' the answer's no deal.'

In his gaze there was a hint of embarrassment. Garbo played on it. 'You can't leave me here.'

'Whit d'ye mean, "here"?' Kern surveyed the three-storey tenements which surrounded the wasteland like the remains of some frontier outworks, their walls thick enough to contain the living rooms of the garrison. 'When I was a kid, we used to come here for holidays.'

A dusty joke which made him smile. Garbo said: 'The least you can do is drop me back at my hotel.'

'Fair enough.' Kern got into the van and opened the passenger-side door. Garbo knew he'd failed a test. Tribal maybe, but crucial. He now had to take advantage of Kern's spasm of humour. 'You know how I'm paying?'

Kern started the van's engine which had enough grunt for a tank. 'I don't care how you're paying, pal, I'm not interested.'

He was when Garbo dropped the net bag of what appeared to be gold-foil wrapped chocolate coins in his lap. He left the engine running to feel carefully among the chocolates and withdraw one which he bit into before holding it up to the light. 'Vicky. Haven't seen one of these since I was in Oman. Beats getting paid in washers.'

The reminiscence was designed to impress Garbo both with its implication of Kern's mercenary service in the Arab Trucial State of Muscat and Oman and his knowledge of the area's favourite currency: Queen Victoria gold sovereigns. Garbo was more taken with the awe in Kern's voice and said: 'There's another forty nine in the bag. Down payment.'

'Down payment nothing! I'm not looking at a job like yours for an upfront of less than ten.' He meant ten thousand pounds. 'Looking at?' Garbo said. 'Or shaking on?'

'Okay. Okay. Shaking on.'

Garbo dropped another net bag in Kern's lap. 'There's another fifty Vickies—an easy ten thousand.'

Kern seemed to agree. He put the bags in the dashboard compartment and then stuck out his hand—etched with machine oil—to shake Garbo's.

'You remember what I need?' Garbo said.

'Not me, pal, I suffer from short-term memory loss.'

Garbo missed the sarcasm. 'Maybe I should write it down.'

'Maybe nothing.' Kern accelerated onto one of the fly-overs which vaulted the city's tenements and streets like the concrete rainbow of a leprechaun hell. 'What kind of bampot do you take me for? Of course, I remember: twelve-bore sawn-off. SMG. Rifle.'

'That's it.'

'Preference on the rifle?'

'Anything as long as it doesn't jam and is accurate.'

'Can do you a Kentucky rifle—drive a nail at fifty yards. Or snuff a candle.'

'Nails I hammer. Candles I blow out. Get me something with a bit of range and a telescopic sight.'

'I'll see what I can do.'

‘Plus ammo.’

Kern sighed. Some remarks were beyond sarcasm. He shut off the van’s engine. They were outside the Central Hotel where Garbo had asked to be dropped. ‘I’ll be needing some *plastique,’* he said.

‘*Plastique*,’ Kern said. ‘Ooh-la-la! Composition 4 or Semtex?’

‘Composition 4. One block. Say a half a pound. Plus detonator.’

Kern sighed again. Hell’s teeth, he thought, I’m beginning to sound like the wife. And said: ‘Some firing circuit wire maybe? Spark box?’

‘Forget the box. Delivery?’

‘A week?’

‘Fine. I’ll call you with an RV.’

‘Here?’

Garbo gave him a look as he got out of the van: *Do me a favour, mate.*

Kern clapped his hands and rubbed them together. If this big Aussie didn’t need a spark box, it could mean he was planning to use an alternative power source for the detonator. Kern restarted the van’s engine. Which could also mean some poor guy was going to kingdom come on something more lethal than wings of song when he switched on **his** engine.

Kern turned left into Hope Street heading for the city’s Southside. Garbo hailed a cab and asked to be taken to the city’s airport. There he collected his vehicle—a beat-up Subaru—and drove west along the road that paralleled the river Clyde.

– 9 –

Rules Restaurant, Maiden Lane, W.C.2

Guthrie had chosen Rules as against Simpson's-in-the-Strand because it was quieter. Like a fragment of an English manor house left over from more idyllic times with traditional servitors, food and wine.

Guy Jessop was only fifteen minutes late. 'Trim at Trumper's.' His thinning blonde hair was indeed burnished with that barber's 'Honey and Flowers', his cheeks still pink from hot towels. His dark, double-breasted flannel suit had a chalk-strip thick enough to have made Al Capone blench. As would the hairier situations in which Jessop had found himself. Jessop being Jessop didn't apologise for his lateness. He evinced alarm. 'You haven't converted, I hope. Not you, my staunch Presbyterian.' He rolled the Rs in Presbyterian as melodramatically as an Englishman with a lisp could.

'Church of Scotland,' Guthrie said. 'Episcopalian.'

Jessop registered mock shock. 'Your hero was an avowed Presbyterian, your hero, James Graham, Marquis of Montrose, whose deeds as Captain-General of Scotland during the Civil Wars you used to extol so boringly. Good lord, as if they'd happened yesterday and not in the seventeenth century.'

'With better fortune Montrose could have turned the tide,' said Guthrie. 'A great soldier.'

'You mean like you rather than me.'

Guthrie ignored the tease. 'A noble spirit. A bridger of religious divisions.'

'In that case, you should remember this is a preferred haunt of Romans. And others.'

Jessop's left eye, puckered by a scar, made him appear to be winking. He indicated a nearby table where a chap in mousy grey, rather mangy velvet and grannie glasses was talking to an Indian in a silvery, raw-silk suit. 'RCs and Parsees,' Jessop said.

'Seriously,' Guthrie said. But he was smiling at Jessop's echo of their sergeant major's church parade command: 'RCs, Parsees, Chinese and Japanese fall out.'

The waiter poured the Barsac Guthrie had ordered to accompany their Vichyssoise. Jessop raised his glass. 'Must be serious if Jock's buying.'

Guthrie said: 'I wish I could afford wine as old as your jokes.'

'Sensitive today, are we? Well, let me tell you I'm still recovering from the mischief you did me at our last reunion.'

They'd been in the same training squad for the 1980 intake of potential guards officers. At their re-union, it was their custom to indulge in drunken versions of the initiative tests they had once undergone with ravines, oil drums and short planks, substituting any available dining room furniture for these hazards and ending up with an all-in, unarmed combat melée. Hence the mischief done to Jessop.

From the guards squad and the Mons Officer Cadet Training Unit, Guthrie had been posted to the Scots Guards and Jessop to the Grenadiers. The coincidence of the military machine had brought them together as guards were changed at Buckingham Palace and as each other's guests in their regimental messes.

More significantly, Guthrie had volunteered for the Special Air Service Regiment and found himself training at douce Hereford and in the gut-wrench, Mars-bar wilds of Wales where Jessop had already been badged as a member of the S.A.S. Guards Squadron. Guthrie passed the initial training-course tests, known as Sickener One and Sickener Two, yet opted not to complete the rest.

Jessop went on to mightier deeds: forward air traffic controller in the Falklands War against Argentine. After the war, he went on the reserve, while undertaking more lucrative civil ventures.

Which was why Guthrie was ordering Nuit St Georges to accompany their rack of lamb and allowing Jessop to continue rolling his Rs atrociously. 'So how are things in the fornication line?'

'As well as can be expected.'

'Is that all? No ecstatic orgasms, then?'

'One lives in hope.'

'Well, it beats fear, I suppose, though not by much.'

'You should know since you're still terrifying yourself.' Jessop smiled. Too smugly. Guthrie jabbed. 'Which is the more fearsome,' he said, 'your S.A.S. exercises or ye olde Masonic rituals?'

Jessop's levity was edged. 'Oh, no, surely not, surely not a Masonophobe? Not you. You did start out on the square. I wonder what changed you.'

Guthrie was not about to tell Jessop and be subjected to another roll of atrocious Rs. He poured more wine and regaled Jessop with the attempted kidnapping of the Queen's piper. He ended with the line: 'They might've have done better if you'd been running the show.'

'Flattery will get you bonked', Jessop said. 'But not by me.'

The voice of the mangy-velvet chap filled the silence. Salesman? Wine? 'Astounding nose,' he was saying. 'Oaky palate. More acorn than trunk if you follow me.' The Indian did, if nodding was still a sign of comprehension.

Guthrie took the Queen's pudding as a cue to mention his reason for the lunch and got a sour answer from Jessop. 'You want me to find you what?' His voice had gone low, and lost its levity.

'A ruffian,' Guthrie said. 'One of your funnies. A hard case. To chastise a sampling of the sub-species, Scribe and Pharisee—journalists, photographers—*pour encouragers les autres.*'

Jessop twirled the glass of Marsala he'd ordered. 'A ruffian, you say, to chastise a sampling of the sub-species, Scribe and Pharisee?'

The sourness left Guthrie undeterred. 'It has to be someone unconnected with the Palace,' he said. 'Someone who doesn't even know who he's doing it for.'

'I should hope not,' Jessop said. 'Sorry, old boy, I'm not your man.'

'You said—at the re-union—your talent organization, the K.M. Agency, right? I assumed *keeni-meeni.*'

Jessop's hearty laugh dismissed the notion that he was into *keeni-meeni*—Swahili for snake in the grass—a term used for the employment of personnel on security and other more covertly lethal mercenary activities. Despite the sweet Marsala, Jessop's sourness did not leave him. 'I do run a talent organisation,' he said. 'Kaleidoscope Management Agency: theatre, films and television. Not to mention advertising commercials—the repertory theatre of the idiot box.' He laughed again and Guthrie laughed with him. 'I was sure.'

'No, you were wrong.' Jessop finished his Marsala. 'Marvellous lunch. A word of advice in return. You're the original *sans peur et sans reproche.*' As Guthrie began to protest, Jessop over-rode him. 'Please, no remonstrances. There are those who believed you bailed out of the S.A.S. course because you couldn't face the shit and pain of the anti-interrogation phase or maybe the interrogation phase. Others—and I'm one of them—know better.'

Guthrie said: 'Coffee?'

'Not if you're trying to interrupt.' Jessop leaned across the table, his puckered eye gleaming. 'You got a whisper your regiment was Falklands bound. Correct? The winged dagger and Who Dares Wins couldn't compete with the ratty old thistle and Who Dares Meddle With Me?

'Wha Daurs Meddle Wi' Me?' Guthrie said. 'Nemo me impune lacessit.'

'Exactly. A soldier scholar like you doesn't want to be playing *keeni-meeni* go-between. You want to command your regiment one day—as your father might have.'

Guthrie's silence was a requiem. His father might've commanded the regiment had he not—uncanny in a man reputedly impervious to shit, shot and shell—succumbed to malaria during an undeclared war in Borneo.

– 10 –

Guildhall Crypt, London, E.C.2

Rex D'Acre's pleasure at being back in the low-vaulted crypt with its squat marble pillars was not unalloyed. Throughout the ancient ritual of the installation of the Worshipful Grand Master of Guildhall Lodge No. 3111, he'd been unable to repress his anxiety at Alisdair Guthrie's failure to procure a ruffian.

Try as he might to concentrate on the ritual—which he himself had undergone as Past Master of his mother lodge, the Lloyds of London lodge, Black Horse of Lombard Street, Lodge 4155—he could not prevent his anxiety increasing.

And his anger.

Not only had Guthrie failed to procure a ruffian, he made it clear he regretted undertaking the task.

Worse.

D'Acre again tried to concentrate on the ritual. It had reached the climactic point when all except Installed Masters had been cleared from the crypt, the point when the secrets of the Chair were being given to the neophyte Grand Master who, having sworn that his right hand could be struck off and slung over his left shoulder, there to wither, should he betray his trust, was being shown the secret grip exchanged by freemasons of his rank left hand on t'other's left shoulder with arms kept straight—and the secret word Giblum as well as the secret Sign of Salutation—bowing and saluting with the right hand from the forehead three times, stepping backwards with the right foot.

Much worse.

Guthrie had added profound—no, profane—insult to injury by saying he should not have accepted the task after the exchange of masonic signs. 'I no longer believe—if I ever did—in all that drebbidge.'

Drebbidge.

The new Worshipful Master was investing his officers, arrayed, as he was, in lambskin aprons lined with garter blue, on their shoulders, embroidered with ears of corn and sprigs of acacia, the tree that betrayed the guilt of the Apprentice Masons, Jubela, Jubelo and Jubelum, in masonic mythology murderers of Hiram Abiff, architect of Solomon's Temple.

In the light of the Guildhall Temple's east, west and north torches, D'Acre surveyed his fellow guests. Distinguished men whose Masonic jewels, glittering ruby, emerald and gold, were meet symbol of their careers and the membership of such luminous lodges as the Bank of England Lodge No. 263, the Chancery Bar Lodge No. 2456, Ad Astra Lodge No. 3808 and Manor of St James Lodge No. 9179.

Distinguished indeed as had been Guthrie's father: Colonel Hector Guthrie, M.C., D.S.O. and Bar, Past Grand Master of Army Lodge 303.

Anger overrode D'Acre's anxiety: anger at Guthrie, anger at himelf. He should've double-checked Guthrie's *bona fides* instead of relying on the United Grand Lodge Year Book listing him as a Lewis—son of a freemason—and an entered Apprentice of Army Lodge 303.

The Guildhall Lodge, given its links with such livery companies as the Cooks, the Grocers, the Bakers, the Poulterers, the Fishmongers and the Vintners, was famous for its hospitality. In the Guildhall dining room, D'Acre was not surprised to find himself seated at the board with a fellow guest. And since it is in the nature of any network to produce coincidences, he was also unsurprised in the exchange of masonic courtesies to find that the guest, Guy Jessop, was a Past Master of Army Lodge 303.

Nevertheless, he was surprised when the firing began—the drinking of toasts with heavy glasses being hammered on the boards to indicate no heeltaps. Under cover of the firing, Jessop said: 'You have problems.'

D'Acre touched his lips with his white linen napkin. 'I have.'

'Let's not waste time in conjugation,' Jessop said. 'Your first problem is called Guthrie—Alisdair of that ilk, and I'm here to help you with it.'

'Your solution?'

'No, no. The solution is not mine. It's yours. Guthrie is an able and ambitious professional. He must be given the opportunity of a role less hedonistic than he is now enjoying. You follow?'

D'Acre did. No one from the lowliest footman to the Queen slept—or did not sleep—with anyone but it was noised abroad in the Palace. So D'Acre knew of Guthrie's bedding of Pamela Fitzgibbon.

Jessop was saying: 'A word in due season—you know the Palace better than I—possibly in the India Room might do the trick.'

Boundless insouciance. While D'Acre was ingesting it with its hint that he should make an approach to the Defence Services Secretary's office, Jessop was going on: 'Your second problem is, I gather, that you need a ruffian. Perhaps Agenda Lodge One can help.'

D'Acre knew his Masonic *Year Book* as he knew his *Debrett* and *Who's Who*. 'Agenda One,' he said. 'That's not a lodge I recall.'

In the life and death poker he played, Jessop believed in bluffing big. That way your antagonist might see a blink as a function of magnitude rather than falsity. 'Not listed,' he said. 'Nor likely to be. Too many of the profane already have access to the Year Book. Given Agenda One's dedication to the defence of the the Realm at all hazard, I think you would agree that caution is of the essence.'

Caution.

A key word in masonic discourse. D'Acre echoed it ritually even there. 'I was taught to be cautious.'

Jessop raised his glass of Chateau Mouton Rothschild—a masonic name to conjure with. 'You were also taught that in distress you should seek the aid of your brother masons.' He drank and hammered his empty glass on the board. 'Agenda One has come to your aid from Grand East.'

'Grand East.'

Buckingham Palace was one redoubt of D'Acre's ambition, the other was Grand East, headquarters of the Supreme Council in Duke Street, St James from which the Royal Arch, the higher, more potent degrees of masonry, were administered. The very thought of thirty degrees beyond the three he already held intoxicated D'Acre more than the Chateau Mouton Rothschild. 'Grand East,' he said. 'Grand East.'

Jessop said: 'I realise you may wish to give this approach due thought but I also understand that the need is rather urgent.'

'You have someone suitable in mind.'

Jessop could do a nice line in shock-horror. 'Not I, oh, no. You misunderstand completely.' The passing of business cards is not covered by masonic ritual yet it is commonplace where masons meet. Jessop passed D'Acre a business card. 'Quarter-master,' he said. 'Supplies ruffians in waiting.'

D'Acre stared at him, ice-eyed, and Jessop realized that D'Acre, like many amateur plotters, had more than a touch of madness in him. He tucked the card into his breast pocket behind his white silk handkerchief, contriving also to lay his right hand, thumb upright, against his breast in the masonic sign of respect.

The speeches and the firing, so eloquent, so thunderous, were dying in slow fumes of port and cigars. His face grim, Jessop drew his right hand, thumb inward, across his throat in the sign of secrecy.

Here he was: a Freemason who whatever the mealy mouthed might say to the profane believed in the full import of the oaths he had taken: as an Entered Apprentice to maintain Freemasonry's secrets on penalty of having his throat cut across, tongue torn out by the root and buried in the sand of the sea at low water mark.

As a Fellow Craft Mason to maintain the secrets on penalty of having the left breast laid open, the heart torn therefrom and given to ravenous birds or devouring beasts as prey.

And as a Master Mason on penalty of being severed in two, bowels burned to ashes and those ashes scattered over the face of the earth and wafted by the four cardinal winds of heaven that no traces or remembrance of so vile a wretch may be found among men, particularly Master Masons.

D'Acre, too, adhered to the spirit of those oaths. He, too, had felt the noose around his neck, the poniard at his left breast and had been raised from the grave by a Master Mason's grip—the grip he was receiving from Jessop: his right thumb pressing between the joints of D'Acre's second and third knuckles.

A pressure D'Acre returned to be rewarded by D'Acre's reciting the five points of fellowship: 'I greet you as a brother' and shifting his foot to meet D'Acre's. 'I walk with you', his knee meeting D'Acre's, 'I pray for you', his chest touching D'Acre's, 'Your secrets are my secrets', his hand on D'Acre's shoulder, 'I will ward off evil from you', following this with the secret word, 'Ma-ha-bo Ma-haf-bif.'

Both in different ways were profoundly moved: Jessop excited, seeing Freemasonry as a tool of his covert trade; D'Acre emotional, seeing Freemasonry as transcendent, a system to enlighten the chosen and bring them to the pinnacles of ambition.

The Lancia was powerful. The music from its stereo system even more powerful: Wolfgang Amadeus Mozart's, *The Magic Flute,* so redolent of masonic myth. D'Acre always played it while driving home after a lodge meeting. He came through the blare and bright squalor of Piccadilly and turned into Duke Street.

The music swooped as he passed the neo-classical facade of Grand East, the Supreme Council headquarters. The music lifted triumphantly carrying D'Acre with it. To become a Freemason, he had been constrained to take the initiative. As a Master Mason he would have to be deemed worthy to ascend from what he'd heard profanely described as the soap opera of the three Blue Lodge degrees to the grand opera of the Red, Royal Arch, degrees administered by the Supreme Council.

The gilded coat of arms on the main gate of Buckingham Palace was caught in the Lancia spotlight. Somewhere an armed sentry stamped his alertness. D'Acre gazed at the floodlit bulk of the palace, location of other honours, trivial by the transcendent standards of Freemasonry yet not without cachet: the Royal Victorian Order. Or better: the Order of Merit, or the Most Noble Order of the Garter.

So beguilingly did *The Magic Flute* combine with D'Acre's imagination that he could feel the weight of the blue velvet garter robes across his shoulders, see his garter plate with all the others in St George's Chapel, Windsor.

Honi soi qui mal y pense. Who would evil think of the man who saved the Royal House of Windsor? Who brought it back to sense that its greatest prop and stay was Freemasonry? Who showed Prince Charles his error in rejecting it? For would he and his wife—so fair, so frail—have had to suffer the slings and arrow of outrageous hacks had he been able to make the grand hailing sign of distress, raising his hands to heaven and uttering the words: 'O Lord, my God, is there no help for the widow's son?'

Yet was Prince Charles wholly to be blamed? His papa, Prince Philip, treated his Entered Apprenticeship in Navy Lodge No. 2612 as more than a sop to his father-in-law George VI. And what of the negative influence of the Queen Mother? Despite her benign demeanor she could be gently ruthless.

D'Acre knew the simple answer to all his questions. He switched off *The Magic Flute* yet its exaltation continued.

And its dread.

For betrayal of Masonic lore, Mozart was reputedly poisoned.

– 11 –

The Cafe Royal, Regent Street, W.1

Inside the entrance, Captain Roy Chilvers, Royal Marines ADC to the Palace Defence Services Secretary was waiting. Dark suit. Presentable enough. Austin Reed, D'Acre guessed. He himself also wore a dark suit: Gieves and Hawkes, Prince Charles' Savile Row tailor. And the Princess Diana's. Her scarlet and gold colonel-in-chief's mess jackets were tailored by the G and H masters. Fetching.

Devastatingly fetching.

Jessop's hint about the India Room had been shrewd enough. D'Acre had refined it to accord with his own rules: never discuss unofficial matters in official surroundings such as the India Room, or the Household Dining Room; always get an underling to convey a matter so that he can present it to his master as his own.

'Lanson, I think,' D'Acre said, naming the Queen's favourite champagne.

Chilver's agreed as D'Acre ushered him to the grill, a red plush and gilt, silver, crystal and damask refuge from the raucous squalor and tawdry commerce of Piccadilly Circus.

A pink-cheeked squire, Chilvers, touch of premature puce that might one day counterpoint red tabs, if his doltish pertinacity was any guide.

Over potted shrimps, he quizzed D'Acre on his feelings about being courted by the households of Prince Charles and the Princess Diana.

This cued D'Acre to a modest disclaimer about the happiness of his current position, and to prove it he retailed an exchange between the Queen and her Prime Minister during their weekly Tuesday evening meeting.

The P.M. D'Acre said, had been bemoaning the lack of close intelligence liaison among the various security units in Northern Ireland: British Army Intelligence, the Special Air Service Regiment, the Royal Ulster Constabulary, its Special Branch as well as MI5 and MI6.

'Yes,' Chilvers said, hacking into his Dover sole, 'there's little love lost between the Green Slime and the Sandy Bandits.' And was delighted to score off D'Acre's civilian puzzlement: 'Intelligence Corps and S.A.S. nicknames, from their beret colours As for dear, old M15 and MI6, in Ireland they're more like Punch and Judy than the Secret Intelligence Service units charged with domestic and foreign funny business.'

D'Acre knew this. His eyes may have glazed. Chilvers went on: 'You were saying? Unblinking, D'Acre took the liberty—and said so—of telling Chilvers how the Queen, responding to the P.M.'s complaint, had said: 'You need our Major Guthrie.'

'The P.M.?'

'Not a word. Nevertheless, his anxiety level, I understand, did drop considerably.'

'I'm not surprised. Such a soother, Her Majesty.'

'Indeed. Quite maternal her attitude to the P.M. Looks at him, I believe, as if she wants to tuck his shirt in properly.'

Chilvers's laughter at this reference to the Prime Minister John Major's reported penchant for tucking his shirt into his underpants made D'Acre certain Chilvers had been hooked with his false fly and would regale his master with the shirt anecdote and more crucially with the Queen's suggestion about Major Guthrie.

Royal commands were for theatricals. In offstage manoeuvres, royal suggestions carried more weight.

D'Acre ordered Hine, Prince Philip's favourite cognac, raised his glass to Chilvers and said: 'To you and Major Alisdair Guthrie. May you both get what you deserve.'

– 12 –

Eaton Mews, London, S.W.1

Naked at the French window of her rented cottage, Pamela Fitzgibbon gazed over the wrought-iron rail at the potted geraniums, red against the white walls of the house across the cobbled lane.

Blood red.

She shivered. 'The geraniums need watering.'

From the bed behind her, Alisdair Guthrie laughed. 'You'll have more than geraniums to water if you'll think seriously about what I've said.'

'My maiden aunt told me never to accept a post-bonk proposal of marriage.'

'Your maiden aunt? Maiden? What would she've known about such proposals.'

'Nothing. She'd been warned, and passed the warning on to me like an heirloom she never needed.'

He laughed again. And was suddenly behind her cupping her breasts and turning her and kissing her and entering her and bringing her strongly to tiptoe pleasure as they moved together back to her bed in the reality of what ballet simulates.

There was wine—Montrachet—olives and cheese on a bedside table. She poured for him. 'You were saying before you rudely interrupted yourself.'

'Bundle and go's the call. Advance Captain Chilvers to take over my position.' He imitated the sound of a bugle. 'Bundle and go.'

'I expected you to be more upset about leaving.'

So had Guthrie who'd taken a last privileged stroll through the Palace to feed nostalgia: the throne room where the Princess Diana was said to have learned to tap dance; the Household Corridor where Edward VII's secretary shot himself; the royal picture gallery once the preserve of Sir Anthony Blunt, who retrieved from postwar Germany the secret Marbug file on the Duke of Windsor's Nazi dealings, while himself a traitor in the service of Soviet Russia.

All those legends. All that silk, scarlet and gilded magnificence. Guthrie was struck by an impression of being in a mausoleum, a fabled tomb like Tutankhamen's or Nefertiti's, arrayed with treasures, attended by retainers, from which he was escaping before he was walled in forever.

'Why?' Pamela Fitzgibbon was saying. 'Why bundle and go? You didn't pick your nose with a silver marrow spoon, did you?'

Palace myth had it that President Ceausescu of Romania had perpetrated this breach of etiquette. Guthrie responded with a reference to another Ceausescu breach. 'The palace whisky, I didn't steal that either.'

He gave her a winey kiss. 'There again, it might've been you. Her Maj takes a dim view of in-house love since my predecessor Commander Lawrence and her daughter. Don't forget his old room was allocated to me.'

'One four two. Surely not? He wasn't given your kind of gong, Lieutenant of the Royal Victorian Order. There must've been something else.'

Guthrie kissed her again. 'Not that I know of.' And after she had returned his kiss. 'Except ... I did something daft.'

'You?'

He told her then about his walk in the palace gardens with Rex D'Acre and his subsequent meeting with Guy Jessop.

'A ruffian?' she said. 'Rex D'Acre asked you to contact a ruffian for him and you went to Guy Jessop?'

'To chastise a sampling of the sub-species Scribe and Pharisee, journalists, photographers, *pour encourager les autres.*'

'But Jessop.'

'I'd heard he was into providing *keeni-meeni*, covert services. He disabused me.'

'Did he now?'

'Quick smart. Simply ridiculous, the whole shebang especially my response to D'Acre's Masonic drebbidge.'

'I thought …' She broke off, aware that her deception was showing, and with it her knowledge of Guy Jessop: he was into keeni-meeni, including tasks more lethal than chastising Scribes and Pharisees. She covered her mistake with the exact truth. 'You didn't tell me you were a Freemason.'

'I'm not, well, not in any real sense. Which I should've told D'Acre, instead of responding to his sign of distress. Why I did, search me.'

She did. 'Lovely kneecaps. And what's this?'

'It's serious.'

'In that case, think ambition, yours, and D'Acre's something of a power broker as well as a Mason.'

'I'm not, I tell you.'

'Not ambitious.'

'No more than the man ahead of me or the man behind: And, yes, D'Acre is a power broker of sorts.'

'Arranging to have Scribes and Pharisees chastised?'

'That's what he said. But he's mask on mask. I wonder if there isn't something else, you know? Some other purpose.'

'A secret. A secret for two little Masons to share.'

'For the last time, I'm not a Mason. I did enter but only to please my father and why he was one, given my grandfather, I don't know.'

'Your grandfather wasn't one?'

'He was until ...'

Guthrie was eager for more than kisses. She said: 'Until?'

'Old story.'

She was moving with him. 'So is this. The oldest, yes? And it does matter. Oh, yes! Yes! And again, yes!'

He broke their silence with the story: his grandfather preparing to embark for Great War active service was watching his soldier-servant packing his kit when a paper fell from the pocket of a tunic.

'The soldier-servant—a MacDonald of the Isles—picked up the paper, glanced at it and then at my grandfather before putting the paper back in the tunic. My grandfather told me he never forgot that glance. I don't think he ever did. In fact, it drove him quite potty. He took to drinking. Vat 69. And after a few drams, he'd try to dial it.'

'Vat 69?'

'The Pope's telephone number, my grandfather used to say. He wanted to tell him about the evils of freemasonry.'

She was not a laugher, Pamela Fitzgibbon. She vented a kind of startled snort of amusement. 'The paper,' she said, 'whatever was it?'

'Same as all paper. Bumph. Special bumph—a Service Certificate no less, issued by my grandfather's lodge, St Andrew's, vouching for the bearer as a worthy Master Mason and commending him for brotherly care and lawful aid to any Mason finding him in distress incident to his service.'

'Well, why ever not?'

'It was printed in various languages including German—.'

'German?'

'Exactly. And Turkish—the languages of the enemy.'

'Still, I don't see that as a reason for going mad.'

'It is if your soldier-servant doesn't have one, your soldier-servant who carried you in under fire after you were wounded by Germans you didn't get a chance to wave your Service Certificate at.'

She did not want him to be aware of how intrigued she was by what he'd told her as well as what he had not: the other possible purpose for Rex D'Acre's move. That could wait.

'You might've kept your little Masonic apron,' she said. 'So sexy, Rather like the kilt.' She kissed his puzzlement into a smile. 'And you a military historian. Don't you remember? Clemenceau's remark when he saw a kilted Scottish unit moving up into the Line. "*Pour l'amour, oui. Pour la guerre, non*".'

Unkilted, un-aproned, he moved to her again to fulfil the part of the epigram about love. She responded. She was also at war, the longest war of the world, a war like a kind of marriage with as much strange love in it as hatred.

– 13 –

Piccadilly Station. London, W.1

From a telephone booth, Rex D'Acre watched rush-hour commuters heading for home. Through the glass of the booth, they had the appearance of undersea creatures. And the circular nature of the station created a sense of a vortex sucking them down to spew them forth again in all the far-flung reaches of the underground system: Heathrow, Ealing Broadway, Uxbridge, West Ruislip, Amersham, Chesham, Watford, Harrow and Wealdstone, Stanmore, Edgeware, High Barnet, Cockfosters, Ongar, Upminister, Island Gardens, New Cross, Wimbledon and Richmond.

He was obeying the instruction on the card Guy Jessop had given him: use a busy public telephone, and was listening to a harsh metallic voice. 'In order to assist you to formulate your requirements, we offer three options.

'Option One: actual bodily harm.

'Option Two: grievous bodily harm.

'Option Three: lethal bodily harm.

'The first two options are necessarily close-encounter. The third option is offered in a) close-encounter mode or b) distance mode. If Option Three is required, please state mode preferred.'

D'Acre hung up: fantasising chastisement of Scribes and Pharisees was one thing, the reality of what he was doing was another. He was sweating coldly. Someone—a woman—was beating on the door with an umbrella like a stubby club. He called again, heard the harsh, metallic voice and said: 'Option Three.' But the voice was saying: 'Our tariff per item is:

'Option One: £25,000.

'Option Two: £50,000.

'Option Three: £100,000.

'Be advised that there is a pro rata additional facilitation and expenses fee of ten per cent on each item. Option One: ten per cent. Option Two: fifteen per cent Option Three: twenty five per cent.

'Fifty per cent of tariff is required in advance. Cash payment or equivalent is essential, that is, bearer bonds, bank certificates of deposit, open letter of credit.

'Method of payment will be notified to you within twenty-four hours of your completed order. Should you decide not to proceed, use the word abort. No refund is possible.'

'You specify time, number of subjects and locations. Security protocols preclude naming of subjects. ID markers are a must. Each factor should be the object of separate calls ASAP. Speak after the tone.'

D'Acre did. 'Option Three,' he said. 'Thank you. Oh, and Mode B.'

The woman who'd been beating on the door—a hundred-proof bottle blonde—wrenched it open. 'How long does it take a chap to tell his wife he's going to be late home for dinner?'

Quandary. D'Acre did not know. Yet. His dream was married life in a royal grace and favour residence. Meanwhile money had more allure than sex. He was dedicating it to a cause with even greater allure: the preservation of a redoubt of civilisation where he could live out his time with some eminently suitable spouse in a semblance of style, order and dignity.

Emerging from the station's Regent Street exit, he was made aware of how great was his need for a redoubt when a teenager wearing a multi-coloured patchwork leather jacket and matching trousers said: 'Fit or a hit, guv. Guaranteed clean—every sodding thing.'

– 14 –

Ocean Drummer, Clyde Estuary

Garbo eased the wheel of his ketch over to take it on a starboard tack as he opened Holy Loch from which a submarine was nosing—whale-bulky, black and sleek like the fulfilment of the legend of the monsters of these waters.

From the sub's fin-like conning tower, a figure waved. In greeting? In warning? Garbo eased the wheel over further to pass well astern. Even so, the ketch lifted and plunged in the powerful wake left by the sub's smooth-seeming passage.

Beside him, Malkie Kern was saying: 'If I'd've known you were going up against a nuclear sub, I'd've fitted a cannon as well.'

In the past week, he'd finished the job of giving Garbo his concealed weapons, insisting only on Garbo's making himself scarce while he did the work at the designated RV: a Greenock fitting-out basin.

Now Kern revealed the reason for his secretiveness. 'Hundred, you won't find them.'

'You're on.'

'Inside an hour.'

Garbo hove to in a curve of the estuary's northern shore, protected from the wind off the wider sea. He operated the self-reefing gear to furl the sails and went for'ard to drop the anchor.

When he returned to the cockpit, Kern had opened the box of food and drink they'd brought and was dismembering a cold roast chicken with his hands. 'Breast or leg?' he said. And at a private tangent. 'What a woman, eh? Grace Kelly. No wonder old 'itchcock went crazy over her. If they'd raffled her, I'd've spent a year's wages on tickets.'

'And got her to help your missus round the house?' Garbo took a leg and a long can of Tennant's lager. 'Okay,' he said. 'SMG's on deck somewhere? Right?' Kern, sprawled on a row of lockers in the cockpit, lifted his can of Tennant's by way of affirmative.

Garbo moved for'ard again, examining the baltic-pine deck planks for signs of new joins. 'Cold,' Kern said. 'And I don't mean the chicken you're scoffing.'

Nothing under the Zodiak rubber dinghy stowed abaft the mainmast. Garbo opened a hatch-cover and surveyed its underside. 'Warmer,' Kern said. 'Garbo stepped into the cockpit and crouched by the auxiliary engine housing. 'Cooking with the wrong fuel,' Kern said.

Garbo opened the lockers and tested their interiors with his fist. No hollow sound from a false back or side. 'My, you're awful clever,' Kern said. Back at the engine housing Garbo began to undo its fastenings. 'Gemme's-a-bogey,' Kern said. The dialect bewildered Garbo 'Time's up,' Kern said. And: 'Come on, pal. Fair's fair. Quarter of an hour each item.'

'Shit, that means I was on a loser no matter what.'

'Make it a hundred each item—then you've got a chance to even things up.'

'Pig's.' Kern took this for refusal and crouched down in front of the central locker. It did have a false back. But to prevent hollow resonance it was padded with foam rubber in which nestled an SMG held by spring clips.

'Magazines,' Garbo said.

The curved 9 mm magazines were hidden in the hollow between the layers of marine ply forming the door. Kern pulled the ring-tab off another Tennant's and dropped it over the side, watching it glinting down through the clear green water past darting curious fish. 'I'll keep a look out here while you try for the other items below—or aloft.'

The ketch's white self-steering vane rising behind his head gave him the appearance of a one-winged angel: a mischievous old boot of an angel.

'Piss off,' Garbo said.

'Aye, aye, Skipper,' Kern said. And proceeded to pee over the side.

Below deck, the ketch was divided into a galley with food storage lockers, a sink, drinking water tank, fridge, and a gas-bottle cooker on gimbals with a swinging drip-tray beneath it. For'ard of the galley was a navigation station with two-way radio, satellite navigation system and chart table.

The main cabin, lined in mahogany and brass, had a centre table under a brass lamp with bunks on either side, decorated with framed, signed pictures of various rock groups and rockers: Bill Haley & His Comets, Rolling Stones, Beatles, Dave Clarke Five, Led Zeppelin, Buddy Holly and The Crickets, Cliff Richard and the Shadows, Eric Clapton, Joe Cocker, Frank Zappa.

At the head of one bunk was a ship's decanter of rum in a teak case. At the head of the other was a bookcase containing a clutch of scrapbooks about rocker exploits, a school-edition of R.L. Stevenson's *Treasure Island* and a shiny, red-bound copy of John Lennon's, *In His Own Write.*

Over the bulkhead doorway leading from the main cabin to the head and the fo'c'sle was a gaudy, electric bass guitar in a moulded plexiglass case. Under it was a brass plate:

PRESENTED TO WILD BILL WEATHERBY BY
HIS FRIENDS 'THANKS FOR THE SESSIONS'

Wild Bill Weatherby, according to the yacht broker who sold the Ocean Drummer, was the greatest session guitarist of them all. 'Never heard of him, you may say,' the broker confided. 'Exactly. Wild Bill was paid to be highly anonymous 'The broker had also confided why Wild Bill's widow was selling the ketch. 'Back taxes. Like John Wayne, the taxman gets you dead or alive.'

There was more Wild Bill junk in the fo'c'sle. Amongst the spare sails, cordage and tins of paint were boxes of rock-'n'-roll publicity shots, records—78s, LPs, CDs—a snare drum with a ruptured skin and a couple of cymbals.

Garbo fossicked, shaking each tin of pain. Only the last didn't make a sloshing sound. Inside, beneath the paint was a white plastic bag knotted at the neck. Inside the bag was a heavy-duty package: the Composition 4 and a smaller plastic package of firing circuit wire.

In the cockpit, Kern was consulting his watch. 'Another hundred you owe me.' Garbo was not a smiler. 'No, we're even on the Comp 4, et cetera, in the paint tin.'

'What do you say to doubling up—two hundred on the next item.'

Below again, Garbo began searching the galley. Kern sat on the companionway steps watching him. When Garbo moved into the navigation station, Kern said: 'You're way off course.' Garbo moved back to the galley. 'Warmer,' Kern said. 'You know I could just go a wee cuppa. Maybe a biscuit or two.' Garbo ignored the request and began to search through the storage lockers. He came upon a packet of chocolate biscuits and threw it to Kern. 'Help yourself.' Kern did not. He laughed. 'Penguins. I'm more into shortbread fingers.'

He came into the galley and began a count-down. When he reached zero, Garbo said: 'All right, you bastard. Where?'

Kern went to the cooker and tilted the drip tray. Its underside was covered with an asbestos pad and clipped to the pad was an under-and-over shotgun, barrels shortened and butt reduced to a pistol grip.

'Cartridges?' Garbo said. Kern replaced the chocolate biscuits in their locker and took out a tartan tin on which was an oval picture of a highlander: eagle-feathered bonnet, plaid, the kilt, white ermine sporran, a brace of horse-pistols at his belt, *sgian dubh* in his hose and a claymore in his hand.

'Delicious.' Kern opened the tin. 'Pure butter shortbread highlanders.' The tin's top layer was indeed of shortbread biscuits. Beneath them, and a layer of bubble plastic, ten shotgun shell were packed flat.

Double 0 buckshot.

'Bellyache in every single one.' Kern rubbed his calloused hands hard enough to generate a fire. 'Okay, okay. I'm feeling generous. Double or quits on the last item.'

The rifle.

Garbo went into the main cabin. Kern obviously had a thing about clipping items. Garbo got down on his hands and knees to search the underside of the table. 'Cold.' Kern said. Garbo looked beneath the bunk mattresses and in the bunk storage lockers.

Kern was singing, 'Oh, where, oh, where has my little gun gone?' His singing was infamous. Garbo'd been told: 'Don't let him start. His grand finale is *Scottish Soldier.* And it'll either make you piss yourself laughing—or want to cut his throat.'

'Oh, where, oh where, can it be?' Kern had one of those cracked voices no amount of grog could lubricate.

'Haven't you got anything better to do?' Garbo said.

He was lifting the hatch that gave access to the bilges. Kern switched to: 'Colder than winter are you ... Garbo's imperturbability was going. No one as small as Kern should be so raucous and cocky. He was bawling: 'Give me an old guitar, a new blue moon and you ...'

Garbo reached down the guitar case. 'Here, play the bloody thing if you must. But no more karaoke.' Kern laughed, took the guitar from its case and handed it to Garbo.

'All right. All right. So where's the rifle?'

'You're holding it, pal.'

Heavy. Garbo examined it closely. The body was of thick solid wood. Red, yellow-tipped flames decorated it and writhed up the stem. He turned it over. The back was flame decorated like the front and enamel glossy. All along the side, up the stem and down the other side a fiery snake writhed. Its spine was a dark, fine line. Got it. Garbo tried to prise the guitar apart.

'Mind the work.' Kern took the guitar and laid it on the table. He unscrewed the tuning knobs on its face, released the tension on the strings and eased the two sections of the guitar apart. The stem of the top section had been cut halfway through where it met the peg area and hollowed out. The bottom section of the stem had also been hollowed out, as had both sections of the guitar's main body. A rifle fitted with telescopic sight and sling lay in the bottom hollow—butt, magazine and sight in the guitar body, barrel in the stem with the sling tucked along the contour of the stem and body.

Kern lifted the rifle. His voice took on a sing-song instructor's tone. 'What we have here: the L42A1 sniper rifle. No. 32 telescopic sight. Based on the .303 Lee Enfield No. 4 rifle, initially modified to take the standard 7.62 NATO round and further modified by yours truly to take a special high-load, max-range 7.62 round. Magazine capacity 10 rounds. Note how the stock has been trimmed by half and that the butt has had the standard cheek piece removed. Note also the special feature.'

While he spoke Kern was demonstrating the feature: the butt had been slimmed and hinged so that it could be folded under the trigger guard.

It was this feature that had deceived Garbo. He had assumed a rifle would be too long for the guitar. Kern snapped the butt into firing position and locked it there with a brass bolt on top of the butt. He handed the rifle to Garbo. 'Cheap at the price, pal.'

Garbo put his arm through the rifle sling before shouldering the weapon and sighting through the companionway entrance to the tip of the self-steering vane where a sea, gull was perched. Kern said: 'She's zeroed. An easy thousand yards. Knock off the pirate chief while he's still trying to spot you.'

Garbo swung the rifle on to Kern. 'Pirate chief?'

Kern did not move. 'Bugger me dead,' he said. 'But use a cock-sock. I don't want to die of AIDS.' Garbo lowered the rifle, refolded the butt and replaced the weapon in the guitar. He noted a separate hollow in the body containing ammo: three chargers, thirty rounds.

'Look, pal.' Kern was saying. 'I'm sorry. Wouldn't mind a wee trip to the Café No Problem myself so I had a dekko at your charts. The courses you've plotted. Cousin of mine, Donny McPhail, engineer, went deep-sea. Container ship. Boarded by pirates. And you won't believe this, Donny swears blind one of them was wearing a Celtic jersey.'

Garbo was screwing the two sections of the guitar together again and re-tensioning the strings. Kern kept trying to mollify him.

'Broke my heart having to carve it up,' he said. 'At first I thought it was a Fender Precision. But now, maybe a one-off. Big. Strong. Even Jimi Hendrix would've had trouble trashing that one. He took the guitar from Garbo. 'I'll give you a real song.' He struck a couple of chords. Tinny. 'Pity we can't plug it in to an amp box.' Garbo did not agree. He went on deck as Kern began to sing: 'There was a soldier, a Scottish soldier…'

Anchor inboard, sail raised, Garbo brought the *Ocean Drummer* round to tack back across to Greenock. All the way, Kern kept reprising, A *Scottish Soldier.*

He joined Garbo when they approached the fitting-out basin wharf. Above them, the setting sun illumined a stone anchor, its stem a cross of Lorraine, memorial to the Free French who had sailed from Greenock during World War II.

Kern had been getting twitchy, glancing at his watch. He caught Garbo's eye on him. It was not an eye to be denied. 'The missus,' he said. 'She gets nervous when I'm late. And the more nervous she gets the more questions she asks. We're talking Perry Mason here.'

Garbo handed him the mobile phone from the pouch on his belt. Kern tapped in his number. 'That you, hen? ... Who do you think it is? It's me–your man.' He looked at Garbo apologetically. 'What am I doing? What else but lining up a wee holiday for you? Where?' He looked at Garbo again. 'Where else but the most beautiful place in the whole, wide world. You can keep Mykonos, Malta, the Costa del Sol, aye, and the Cote d'Azur. Costa Clyde's the place. How does Dunoon sound to you? ... Right. Right. An hour at the most.'

He did a pretend waltz as he handed the mobile back to Garbo. 'Loves Dunoon, loves it, the missus. We had our honeymoon there. Now that's living, honeymoon in Dunoon. Must be winter, mind. That way your bride doesn't have an excuse to do anything but what you want.'

Kern's battleship-grey van was parked near the fitting-out basin. He was disappointed when Garbo paid him the other half of the contract in banknotes not gold. He cheered up when Garbo added the amount of their bet to the fee.

From the van's glovebox he took a half-bottle of whisky *Highland Nectar,* and held it out to Garbo who took a swallow of it. Kern took a longer swallow after intoning: 'Here's tae us. Wha's like us. Damn few.

An' they're a' deid.'

He started the van's engine. 'By the by, I've been meaning to ask, why Greenock?' Garbo shrugged. Kern said: 'Okay, okay, I owe you the bottom half of the next bottle you buy.' As he turned on to the main road and headed for home, the van backfired once.

Like a portent.

– 15 –

Red Hand Farm, County Armagh

Rising and falling on tides of pain and unconsciousness, Alisdair Guthrie'd been aware of being carried, slung over someone's shoulder. Uncannily, he'd imagined himself to be his grandfather being brought in under fire by his soldier-servant. That was before the roaring impact came back to him, the roaring impact on the chopper.

Mortar bomb?

Red Eye Rocket?

The roaring impact and the whirling metallic cacophony mixed with the flesh-and-blood yells of the fifteen-strong Joint Mobile Patrol of Royal Ulster Constabulary and British infantry, squatting on their steel helmets because balls were more important than brains.

He had been near a side door, surveying the terrain through night-vision binoculars. How green, how weirdly green, was Ireland, he'd been thinking when the roaring impact threw him fully equipped from the chopper into blackness.

Now he was naked, hooded and surrounded by stench. A stable? A byre? And where? Bandit country. Or maybe even over the border, a line drawn temporarily in ink and more permanently in blood.

'Who are you?' Irish voice with the hammer-on-anvil vowels of the north. 'And what're you doing here?'

Time, Guthrie knew, was his friend, his interrogator's enemy. 'I might ask you the same questions. Who're you? IRA—Provo? Official?

Irish National Liberation Army? Or Ulster Defence Association? Ulster Volunteer Force? Ulster Freedom Fighters?'

'Mick's Own. And I'm Mick. So who are you and what're you doing here?'

'Where?' Guthrie said. 'Where is here?'

The blow that slammed against the side of his head was open-handed. 'Never mind that. Just tell me who you are.'

This question, Guthrie realised, was superfluous. His ID had been with his equipment and had been taken. Completely superfluous—unless Mick suspected the ID was in a cover name.

If so, Guthrie knew, he could not give his real name. It could link him to the Palace. Its security. She was there. Pamela Fitz. And the Queen—the Forlorn Hope. Guthrie said: 'UFF, right? Impressed. Most impressed by one of your wall paintings. Noble scroll. Noble words.' He hesitated . . . '"It is in truth not for glory nor riches nor honour . . . "' He hesitated again. *Must spin* it *out.* And Mick picked up the quotation. '"... we are fighting but for freedom—for that alone, which no honest man gives up but with life itself".'

'UFF,' Guthrie said. 'I knew it.'

'Did you now? And by the same token I suppose you know the document quoted is the Shankhill petition addressed to the bold anti-Pope himself, the Reverend Ian Paisley, and never the Declaration of Abroath, addressed to Pope John the Twenty Second in 1319 as Supreme Pontiff of the Holy Roman and Universal Church by representatives of the Scots who were having their troubles with the English and sent it to the Pope as their arbiter, aye, and with devout kisses of his blessed feet.'

'IRA,' Guthrie said. 'You're IRA—Rah.'

'I told you. Mick's Own.'

'New unit, right? Objective: get the Brits out, leaving rival elements to sort each other out on a clear killing field.'

Mick's laugh was more of a growl. 'You've tapped into a grand nightmare there.' Guthrie was conscious of his leaning close. 'We don't have the white noise here or any of the other refinements of Her Majesty's Castlereagh Interrogation Centre in beautiful downtown Belfast. You'll save us a lot of trouble, and yourself a lot of pain, by giving us your real name.'

Us. Real Name.

Mick had a least one helper. And they knew his ID was cover

'You've got my ID,' Guthrie said. 'What about yours?'

'Questions are ours to ask, yours to answer.'

'My answer is if you're republicans, you're on the wrong side. The Irish are naturally monarchists. Remember the High Kings of Tara. And if you're a Ned, you're named after Edward Bruce, king for a time of Ireland as his brother Robert was King of Scots.'

'Say no more, you gabshite.' No blow came with the order. Guthrie went on. 'You rallied to James II and lost at Boyne Water as you rallied again to his son Prince Charlie and lost again, covering the retreat of the Scottish clans at Culloden.'

'Do you tell me so? Well then, I'll grant you we didn't sell out our king like the English plutocracy and hire a Dutch shirt-lifter and call it a Glorious Revolution, its latest heir, Charles the Every Ready to excuse His Royal Self for breaking his word, before God, to husband his wife.'

'Impudence.'

'Impudence, is it? Wasn't his forebear, James II, mocked from three kingdoms for fealty to his faith? And didn't his namesake Bonnie Prince Charlie drink himself to death for shame of having forfeited his destiny. Shirt-lifter Billy to Tampon Charlie, plutocrat choices both.'

Plutocracy. Plutocrat. Old line IRA with Marxist leanings?

'You make my point,' Guthrie said. 'It's your Presbyterian Irish who're republican at heart. And would be in reality if the Orange

Lodge hadn't been established to pull them from their radicalism. French variety. *Liberté. Egalité. Fraternité.* You know? Bureaucracy. Bourgeoisie. Bugger you Jacques you didn't attend the *Ecole Normale Superieur.* The Orange Lodge is still a bulwark against radicalism, reinforced by its early exemption from the Northern Ireland laws against unlawful oaths and assemblies as the Catholic Church is reinforced by its special position in the Republic of Ireland Constitution.'

The blow this time was from a fist. 'Enough of your trying to Scherezade us.'

Guthrie feigned unconsciousness and was slapped out of it. 'Kings,' he said. 'The Irish achieved more in service to kings than any republic. Wellington knew that when he pushed for the passing of the Catholic Emancipation Act. He knew that at least half his troops in the Napoleonic wars were Irish. 'We must confess, my Lords, that ...' This time when Guthrie hesitated, Mick did not—or could not—pick up on the quotation. He fisted Guthrie again. But Guthrie went on: 'without Catholic blood and Catholic valour no victory could ever have been obtained and the first military talents might have been exerted in vain.'

Mick fisted him again. 'Real name?'

'My ID, you've got. I presume you can read?'

'That we can. You're no more a lieutenant than I'm a field marshal though I've the belly for the rank and you don't for yours. Too much high living on you for a fresh weaned lieutenant.'

Guthrie's feet and hands were bound. He could do nothing when he felt the metal bite into his scrotum. Crocodile clips? Mick said: 'We may not have the refinements of your system but your know-how we have that, and a twelve-volt battery that fell off an Army truck.'

'Read my ID.'

'Give him a jolt,' Mick said. And: 'My apologies. It's Pat that'll be doing the jolting. Say "Hello", Pat.'

Pat did not say hello. He did give Guthrie a jolt that sent an arching scream through his body.

'Nothing like,' Mick said, 'hearing an Englishman warming up to sing.'

'Scotsman,' Guthrie said.

'Lieutenant I might be persuaded to believe,' Mick said. 'But a Scotsman called Percy. Never.'

'Borderer,' Guthrie said, the reply becoming a scream when a second jolt hit him.

This time his scream was echoed by the squeal of a pig.

Not a stable.

Not a byre.

A pigsty.

Mick was saying: 'Wheesht, Billy. We know you're hungry but don't you fret, you'll get yours. Never fear.' A third—and longer—jolt arched through Guthrie. 'Real name?'

'How many times?' Guthrie said. 'How many times do I have to tell you what's on my ID.' And got four jolts which slid together in a single scream.

'Real name?'

'Percy! Percy! Percy!'

And all the time the pig was squealing.

'Poor Billy's hungry for something special,' Mick said. Guthrie was conscious of the crocodile clips being removed and of a sensation of warm pleasure. Through the stink of the pigsty and the stink of himself filtered—it couldn't be—the scent of honey.

Mick said: 'Quite the English aristocrat, aren't you, Billy?' The pig snorted. Mick went on: 'Nothing our Billy likes more than grilled honey balls.'

Guthrie felt himself being lifted. Shoulders and feet. They were going to dump him in a pen with a ravening pig.

Bluff? Like similar bluffs involving hungry dogs on the S.A.S. anti-interrogation course. Was Mick ex-S.A.S., as the IRA's original commander, James Connolly, had been ex-Royal Scots? 'Wait,' Guthrie said. 'Wait.' They halted. 'Walker,' he said. 'Kenneth. Major. Intelligence Corps.'

'Previous posting?'

'Ministry of Defence.'

'Liar.' Mick yelled. Guthrie felt himself being moved again. 'Liar.' This time Mick's voice was muted in mid-yell. He'd heard something. Now Guthrie heard it, too—the blessed clatter he'd been waiting for, the clatter of a reaction chopper grid-searching for him.

'We'll have to head him,' Mick said. Guthrie was dropped to fall among shit and straw. He heard the sound of a pistol being cocked. His own Browning nine-milly? 'No hood,' he said.

Courage can awe cruelty. The hood was removed. Guthrie found himself kneeling before a pit hacked into the earth beneath the flag-stoned floor of the pigsty. He looked up at his captors. They were still hooded. But the courage of his look compelled them to take off their hoods. He knew their faces: hard, grim, true Ulster men, resolute for death.

In his mind, Guthrie had been with such men, men of his hero Montrose's Scots and Irish army, caught between superior enemy armies ready to make a slaughter house of the Bible in the winter of 1645; turned in the night; force marched over snow-choked mountain passes for a surprise attack on rear foes and the rout of them at dawn and Inverlochy.

Not his Browning, the pistol, a silenced Walther 7.65 and Guthrie could feel its muzzle pressed into the base of his skull. Mick said: 'If ye've a prayer, Jock ...'

Guthrie did have a prayer. And even with the reaction chopper beating ever closer, they let him finish it.

And say his last words.

Neither the prayer nor the words prevented the firing of the Walther. Its hollow-point round blew his brains and most of his face, grey and pink, into the pit. His tortured body followed.

The chopper was hovering, a hawk waiting for prey to break from cover. Mick lit a cigarette and began to fork manure and straw mixed with earth on top of the body.

'Would you not do that?' Pat said.

'What?'

'You know I hate it.'

Mick blew smoke. Pat threw a handful of manure at him. 'Put that in your pipe,' he said. 'Brigade intelligence isn't going to be chuffed we didn't break him.'

'Aye, maybe,' Mick said. 'There again, it's my understanding HQ was after corroboration of something, amplification, you know? Not fresh gen.'

The chopper was moving away. Pat tucked the Walther into the waistband of his corduroy trousers and moved to help Mick who was replacing flagstones over the pit.

'Corroboration,' Pat said. 'Amplification. So it was something they already knew. What might that be?' Mick was silent. Pat went on: 'It must've been damnation important for us to down a chopper in hopes of getting him.'

Over the replaced flagstones, Mick was spreading manure and straw. Poor Jock. It's the Last Trump he'll have to wait for, no sniffer dog'll ever raise him.'

'Would you stop your teasing, man,' Pat said. 'What was it?'

'Something Jock was on to, something we couldn't let him know for fear of tipping our source.'

'That's why—I wondered—that's why you took the long way round about his real name.'

'Something about hiring a ruffian.'

'A ruffian,' Pat said. 'Haven't they got an army of them already? What would they be wanting with just the one?'

'The word is to thump newspaper gabshites.'

'Make it half a dozen, and I'll lend a hand.'

'So would I. So would I,' said Mick. 'Can't see it.'

'Aren't the English an outrage on all the world?' Pat spat on his hands and rubbed them together as if he were washing them, and not only to cover any traces from his killing shot. 'I'm glad,' he said. 'I'm glad we didn't get time to feed Jock's balls to the pig.'

'So's the pig.' Mick bent to scratch the pig between its ears. 'Aren't you, Billy?'

'How so?'

'A Jock's balls are a hard chew.'

Their exchange begot a silence. Into the silence, into the moral stench of the sty drifted the memory of Guthrie's prayer, the prayer of his hero, Montrose, composed by him on the eve of his being hanged, drawn and quartered for treason.

'Let them bestow on ev'ry Airth a Limb
'Open all my Veins, that I may swim
'To thee my Saviour, in that Crimson Lake;
'Then place my par-boil'd Head upon a Stake;
'Scatter my Ashes, throw them in the Air;
'Lord (since Thou know'st where all those Atoms are)
'I'm hopeful, once Thou'lt recollect my Dust,
'And confident Thou'lt raise me with the Just.'

As they left the sty, the prayer haunted them like the incense and innocence of their childhood.

The prayer, and Guthrie's own last words: 'Sir Jesus, forgive us all.'

– 16 –

Golden Square. London, W.1

At his desk in the Kaleidoscope Management Agency office, Guy Jessop listened to D'Acre's voice mail: time, location, subjects, ID markers and wiped the mail. Now all he had to do was order up a five-slash-thousand man. Easy. Like hell.

He scrolled through the list of names on the screen of the Apple Mac perched on the Regency desk: headliners, he called them in his showbiz cover jargon—specialists capable of putting the required killing shot into a five-inch diameter circle at up to one thousand yards.

Pity Rex D'Acre hadn't ordered Option One or Option Two: any number of tear-aways available to dispense actual or grievous bodily harm. At bargain rates, too, increasing the profit margin. Five-slash-thousand men were rare and knew their worth.

He crossed to the drinks table near the green leather club couch. Bit early for a snort. There again, no the point in being your own boss if you couldn't break your own rules.

On the way back to his desk, he switched on his telephone recorder and listened the hiss of the wiped tape. D'Acre's call'd been switched from a self-destruct telephone-linked tape-recorder. Funny little place in Hornsey: two-up, two-down with a coin-operated phone in the hallway.

Who'd ha' thought it? Rex D'Acre initially required a ruffian to chastise Scribes and Pharisees. Now he specifies an assassin. Jessop sipped at his pink gin. Cool market player, D'Acre, and with the loot to prove it. Yet there'd been something cracked, in his voice as there had been something mad in his manner at the Guildhall.

Touch of palace lunacy. Jessop himself had passed through those gilded halls. His temptation: to press the silk damask walls to make sure they weren't padded. Yet that had been in the relatively sane period when Prince Charles was still on the delightful duty of getting an heir and spare on the divine Diana, the period before prince and princess decided to wash their monogrammed linen in public. Little wonder, in the current situation, that a courtier like D'Acre should go as barking mad as a royal corgi in pursuit of a palace rat.

The showbiz work names Jessop had given his headliners glowed on the Apple Mac screen.

Negri.

Fine shot. None better. Not available; across the pond in the United States, doubtless being briefed for a C.I.A. black-bag operation.

Swanson.

Almost as fine as Negri. Jessop tapped out a Paris telephone number. The voice that answered was low, slow, controlled. Shit, not hung-over, Jessop thought. And said: 'Swanson?'

'Yeah. it's the old Kennedy-bonked Gloria speaking.'

Not hung-over. Pissed as a newt. 'Are you free for a headliner date? Top fee.'

'When?'

'To be notified. Soon.'

'If that means time to get rid of the shakes, I'm your man.'

Not just pissed. So far gone he wasn't even trying to conceal he was pissed.

'You're not my man.' Jessop hung up. He tapped the Apple Mac keys to erase Swanson from his books. Ex-American paratrooper. Ex-

Foreign Legion, ditto. Who'd ha' thought it? There again, the French drove everyone to drink, including themselves.

Jessop highlighted the name Garbo. No. His message was too demandingly bolshie after his previous task. Anyway it was also too soon, although Garbo's coping with the unexpected complication had been elegant enough to win love-pact, murder-suicide headlines. Not only in the tabloids. The heavies dug up a trick-cyclist to say murder-suicide was as Australian as the *crime passionelle* was French, the grubby sex crime was British and the drive-by killing American.

Pickford.

Jessop tapped a New York number. To the secretary who answered the phone, he said: 'Kaleidoscope Management for your boss.'

'Say again.'

Jessop said again.

'He's in a meeting and cannot be disturbed.'

Jessop said he would ring back in fifteen minutes. He did. His man was still in a meeting. 'Tell him, it's urgent.'

Pickford came on the line. He was breathless. Jessop had no difficulty in deciding the kind of meeting Pickford was party to. 'Still taking care of the hard problems yourself,' he said, and repeated his offer of a headliner date.

'Not interested. Other business commitments, you understand.'

Jessop did. Pickford was ex-SO 13—anti-terrorist squad. He had made a career as an instructor to special weapons squads throughout Britain. 'Winnie's Boys', he nicknamed them—a reference to Winston Churchill calling out Scots Guards riflemen in the 1920s to deal with an anarchist called Peter the Painter. Pickford's other business was real estate in which he was as ruthless as he was with a rifle. 'That pad you mentioned last time we spoke. I've got a place for you on the Upper Eastside. Absolutely right for you. Super security, newly decorated and you—you won't believe it—rent controlled.'

Jessop himself was not one to miss an opening. 'I'd be able to make up my mind on that kind of thing quicker if I weren't pre-occupied with an immediate problem. The fee's absolutely tops. Trio. Up-front seventy-five. Plus appropriate expenses. Money's all ready.'

It was. He'd collected it in a suitcase from the Savoy Hotel cloakroom with a ticket sent to him *poste restante*, Kingsway. Three hundred thousand in fees. Plus seventy five thousand facilitation and expenses fees.

'Seventy-five for a trio,' Pickford was saying. 'Back end the same?'.

'As you say.' Jessop began to hope. 'Expenses also up front to cover trio—say ten.'

Pickford laughed—and the satellite link sent his laughter bouncing eerily into space. 'You know me, business before pleasure.' Whoever was with Pickford seemed to disagree. The last sound Jessop heard before he broke contact was the slop of a water bed.

Remembering phone-traffic monitoring of successive foreign calls, Jessop rang Emma and told her he was thinking of bringing Toby Raeburn home to dinner.

'We have an agreement,' she said. 'I get three months convalescence between his visits. He was here last month and I'm only half recovered from terminal boredom.'

'He's involved in a new venture.'

'How can someone who's been everywhere, met everyone and told everyone all about it have a new venture?'

'Power braces. He's manufacturing them.'

'Not those horrible red-felt things.'

'Reddish. But not felt. He has acquired a job lot of scarlet tunics and is recycling them as braces.'

'No. Absolutely no. And that other sound you heard was my little foot stamping.'

‘Oh, very well. May have to buy him a drink.’

‘Again, no. If you buy him a drink, he will offer to drop you off here and once he sights our front door, you will not be able to stop him coming in and once he gets a sniff of dinner—veal Marengo by the way—you won’t be able to stop him joining us. And you know my father is bidden.’

The thought of her father and Toby Raeburn volleying and thundering at each other was too much even for Jessop. ‘You win,’ he said. And peered at the Apple: Ulanova. He tapped in a Moscow number.

The reply was instant and as clear in tone as it was confused in meaning—a stream of Russian and a background of celebration against which Jessop’s repetition of ‘Kaleidoscope Management, London calling,’ seemed inconsequential. Then out of the confusion came a voice of astonishing politeness and clarity. ‘Ulanova here. What is it you wish?’

Jessop told him.

Ulanova said: ‘Your timing is most unfortunate. Had you rung me yesterday, I would seriously have considered your proposal. Today—today, I celebrate.’

‘Well, done. Many happy returns. Or whatever.’

‘Is not my birthday I celebrate. It is my appointment as a state executioner.’

‘Oh,’ Jessop said. ‘In that case, congratulations.’

He could say no more. He hung up, overwhelmed by one of those helpless fits of laughter that seize men in risky places. What, he wondered, was the difference for the ex-Spetznaz Ulanova between private executioner and state executioner? An apparatchik pension?

The next name on Jessop’s list was Dusé. He tapped in a Milan number. Duse, ex-Bersagliere, had represented his country at the

Olympics in the biathlon event: ski-ing and shooting. No chance of him turning down the booking because of, his appointment as a state executioner. In effect, he already was.

No reply.

Jessop hung up. Garbo? No way.

– 17 –

St. Paul's Cathedral, London, E.C.4

Birton—Jack, photo-journalist—sighted his Pentax into the cathedral sanctuary from the railed balcony high under the dome.

What a position. If only he'd been up here on Charlie Chester and Di Spencer's wedding day instead of outside perched on his step-ladder with a berk of a reporter so piss-weak he couldn't stop the ladder wobbling. Still, he'd got one good shot: Di ducking her head in that shy way of hers.

He took a shot of a cleaner with a mechanical mop drawing wet arcs across the sanctuary's black and white tessellation. Birton was never without at least two cameras:, Pentax loaded black and white, Nikon colour. Birton himself preferred black—a preference going back to when his local newspaper exes weren't elastic enough to stretch to many clothes. Usually, he wore black T-shirts and jeans with an anorak. Today he was toffed up: black tussore Honkers suit, black shirt and boots. He moved back against the curved wall of the dome to get a shot down the cathedral nave.

'Here!' The whisper was ghostly yet commanding. Birton, startled, swung round keeping the camera to his eye. In his viewfinder was Rex D'Acre, elegant in grey Prince of Wales check, blue shirt and red bowtie. He was carrying a Trilby and a rapier-rolled umbrella. His whisper came to Birton again. 'Here!'

Birton altered his focus and knocked off his shot. What's he think

I am, he thought. One of the royal corgis? Ought to pee on his shiny shoes. 'Wotcher, Rex,' he said.

D'Acre winced. Cockneys emphasised their origin in a royal milieu. Seemed to think of the Royal Family as essentially Cockney in the way Romans thought of the Pope as essentially Roman.

Creep hounds, every one with something sinister in the way they debauched the royal mystique for a mess of pix. Yet they did enjoy a weird intimacy with the female royals. The way crimpers did. 'You're looking fit,' D'Acre said. He led Birton past a freshet of Japanese tourists and downstairs. 'Leaving the *Daily Terror* has obviously agreed with you.'

'Fit?' Birton said. 'I'm knackered. What's more, I didn't leave the *Terror*, it left me.'

D'Acre peered at him. 'Yes, you do appear to have acquired a few white hairs.'

'Pissed on, wasn't I? Birton touched the white streak that flashed in his swept-back black hair. 'Pissed on by Captain Bob. From a great height, I can tell you. Gets out of his helicopter on the office roof, he does, and pisses over the side as usual. And there I am heading for a drink in *The Stab*. Sod him.'

'What a perfectly dismal matching of fact and metaphor,' D'Acre said. Birton looked at him as he was inclined to look at reporters. D'Acre said: 'I meant that so many newspaper types were pissed on metaphorically when Maxwell made use of pension funds to finance his ill-fated conquests. Dreadful fellow. My father used to read Beachcomber in the *Daily Express* aloud at the breakfast table. Remember Captain Foulenough?'

Birton nodded. It was easier with someone who rabbited on like D'Acre, 'Foulenough, I believe was a prophecy of Maxwell—Jan Ludwig Hoch—battlefield hero wrapped in business enigma wrapped in all-round monster. I can see him on the last day, rising from his grave in Jerusalem and saying: 'Mine. All mine.' The immortal Rupert standing beside him saying: 'Sorry, sport. Mine. The Hun, the Vandal, the Goth, the Visigoth, the Aussie. And the worst of these is the Aussie.'

Birton shook his head just for the hell of it. D'Acre said: 'Perhaps I'm being too hard. Poor little chap thrown into the deep end of debt early in life and condemned to dog-paddle in it forever, with banker sharks circling.' Birton nodded. He'd been hoping D'Acre would shout him lunch. No chance. He strolled in the cathedral as if they were simply tourists having an irreverent chat. 'How are you finding independent photo-journalism as compared to staff photography?'

Surprised to hear something he could answer, Birton said: 'Staff photography's never that simple. Photo-journalism? The big plus is it only means writing longer captions without some nong of a reporter hanging about calling you his monkey and leaning his ratty copy against your pix.'

D'Acre turned and looked back at the sanctuary. 'The market seems to be holding for pictures of the royal variety.'

'Holding? It's all blue sky. Sometimes ... 'Birton drew a mobile phone from inside his jacket and tapped in a number. 'Any lunch-time calls? ... Fine.' D'Acre registered the phone call, not the lunch hint.

'Sometimes,' Birton said. 'No offence. Sometimes I wonder if it's not like the stockmarket before a crash. Prices are totally incredible. One hundred, two, three, four hundred thousand. Even five. And that's just for covered. Topless. Well, name your price, and bring a wheelbarrow to carry the loot to the bank.'

'What about bottomless—your own speciality?'

Birton was so taken aback at D'Acre's knowledge, he sat down in the nearest pew. Cheeky sod. How did he know about that? His most shameful secret. Mad. He must've been. Mad for the jackpot shot, back in the happier days when Charlie Chester would a-wooing go, stalked by long-lens cameramen in the heather around Balmoral.

Birton'd knocked off a shot of Charlie and his then inamorata frolicking so blithely that his kilt was up. The classic jackpot shot. Not classic enough for the bold Jack Birton. Darkroom magic enabled him to contrive a peek of the royal crown jewels.

The caption writer—Tony What's-His-Name, Oxford, Newdigate Poetry prizewinner—was already in sonnet mode when a picture editor—git, Henry Elfrey, he hadn't graduated yesterday—checking a proof of the pic through his magnifying glass—sussed it had been doctored.

Funny thing about hacks. No worries about conning readers. But they got pissed off—absolutely and bleeding totally—when one of their own tried to con them.

D'Acre'd taken the pew behind Birton. Someone was playing Bach on the cathedral organ, a fugue, weaving celestially among the earthbound pillars and arches, reminding D'Acre of Prince Charles and Princess Diana's wedding day. Dame Kiri Te Kanawa singing, 'Let the Bright Seraphim'. He leaned towards Birton. 'You're missing the boom.'

'Don't tell me. I know. I know. I get only what I can snatch.'

'Ah, yes, of course. When the *Terror* left you, you lost your palace accreditation.'

Birton rose from the pew and headed towards the main door. D'Acre ranged himself alongside. 'Current palace thinking is that staff photographers might well benefit from more freelance competition and independent syndication of photographs, particularly from a freelance with an inside source.'

Birton stepped ahead. 'You're saying you can get me re-accredited? Steer me right?'

‘That depends.’ D’Acre’s eyes were steady yet deceptive.

Sly sod, Birton thought. Finally he gets to the point and it’s the same old point: gelt. ‘How much?’ he said.

D’Acre’s face grew more austere. ‘I hope I don’t understand.’

‘Your cut,’ Birton said. ‘How much—ten per cent, fifteen or the good old McCormack—twenty-five? D’Acre rounded Birton and was down the cathedral steps when Birton caught up with him. ‘So you don’t want a cut. One thing: no bodgie-conk shots.’

D’Acre realised that Birton was seeking to compensate for his previous lapse but wasn’t quite sure what he meant and said so. ‘You’re not quite sure,’ Birton said. ‘Well, I am. Choice of pix—sure sign of any newspaper’s true stance. And the word’s out that bodgie-conk shots of Di are in. I’ve seen them. You get Di profile with the light right for you—wrong for her, poor cow—and she can look like the Wicked Witch of the West End. Or get her front on and she’s a featherweight whose schnoz has been swiped by leather once too often. So no bodgie-conk shots. Right?’

‘Nothing, I can assure you, nothing is further from my mind than bodgie-conk shots.’ D’Acre uttered the last three words like a hungry man chewing on a pork sausage he suspects may be tainted. ‘Moreover I’d as lief you did not refer to Her Royal Highness, the Princess of Wales as a poor cow.’

His rapier-furled umbrella rose like an exclamation mark. ‘Surely it might have occurred even to you that I was seeking the shot—the definitive shot—which shows once and for all what their Royal Highnesses truly mean to each other.’ D’Acre hesitated. ‘A shot of him or of her. No matter.’

A cab drew into the kerb. Birton knocked off a Nikon colour shot of D’Acre getting in. Blew that chance, he was thinking. Imagine a cold kipper like Rex D’Acre being so touchy about Di. There again, no denying she was a darling, fit to give a corpse a hard-on. Except for her schnoz. Not like poor Charlie. He could be difficult. His skin. It always looked as if it'd shrunk in the bath. Too small for him. Especially around the face.

Fleet Street: The Street of Adventure. Or Debenture, as a finance writer Birton once worked with had called it. He eyed the trash-bazaars. Strange how pic-worthy they looked in Bangkok, KL, Honkers or Singapore. Maybe it helped to be jet-lagged. Or lunched.

Sod Rex D'Acre, him and his high-mucka-muckery about Rupert Murdoch being in debt and calling Maxwell, Foulenough, Not that he wasn't. Unsinkable. Belly-up, even in the Med carrying a deadweight of debt. D'Acre wouldn't know about being in the red. More of a lender. Made a difference, which end of the debt stick you were on. The shitty end, or the other. So Rupert was at the shitty end. Not a bad geezer.

Better.

A terrific market.

El Vino: Birton hesitated before going in for a sherry. Quiet one. The wine-bar once resonant with the clash of egos, the ripping of reputations and the throb of gossip too strong for print, had a forsaken air—a theatre from which the first-class repertory company had departed, leaving only strays.

A couple of these were standing at the bar. The taller—wizened character from *Planet of the Apes* with a blonde wig—bestowed a glance on Birton. As a photographer, Birton knew that kind of glance; it expected a full stare of recognition in return. Sorry, Birton thought, must've missed your fifteen minutes of fame wherever. The smaller guy—bright, assured, incisive—was saying: 'You didn't really expect him to turn up.'

'Pillock. One thing's certain. You won't be writing his obituary.'

'Which reminds me. Yours. Was it fifty-eight or fifty-nine, I gave you your TV break?'

Birton ordered another No. 4 sherry, and to get out of hearing and eye-contact moved into the backroom. A mistake. Rex D'Acre was there. Rex D'Acre and Simon Delamere. Not so simple Simon. Still padding himself as well as his expenses. Fat git. So piss-weak he couldn't hold a stepladder steady. On the rise, the git. Simon Delamere and Rex D'Acre. Lunching. Birton exited quickly. Not quickly enough. Behind him, he heard Delamere cry, 'Cock-a-doodle-do!'

That cry, that voice half-Irish, half-posh and all sarcasm, had haunted him like chalk on a squeaking blackboard ever since his effort to enhance Charlie Chester's crown jewels.

Birton swallowed the No. 4 sherry like a medicine. But he knew it was not going to cure the shame he felt at Delamere's cry. And what was Rex D'Acre up to, lunching Delamere, and not him? Salt-beef sandwich time. He settled—like the rest of the universe—for a Burger. Gastro-catastrophe. The only cure was alto-catastrophe. He headed towards the leadlight windows and ye olde timber of the Wig and Pen.

Ahead of him, studying the antique Spy caricatures in the front window as if they were contemporaries, were the El Vino pair. The smaller was saying: 'My point—and I put it forcibly—is that wigs and gowns are an essential part of the court process. They ... what was I saying?'

'I think you were going to say something about distinguishing the lawyers from the crooks.'

'Was I?'

In the autumn sunlight with a shiver of rain in it, Birton realised that the pair were Artful Dodgers become old codgers. If he had another drink, he would end up talking to them and fall into his anecdotage like them instead of pushing on for the jackpot shot. He'd show that git, Simon Delamere. He'd show them all.

The Rapix Worldwide Syndication office was between Holborn and Fleet Street in Chancery Lane. The building leaned towards Lincoln's Inn Fields, and Birton, climbing three flights of stairs, felt as if he were on a listing ship. Outside his office he paused. Not for breath. For inspiration. He'd gone to his meet with D'Acre optimistic. Now he had to think of something not completely negative to tell his partner, Connie Gaudren. He entered his office.

Connie was at the word processor, fingers pattering on the keys at 80 wpm. Plait of long hair coiled in a coronet. No smile.

'How did it go?'

'Very positive. Of course, I—we've—got rules. No point in being a push-over is there? Lowers the price. I mean he saw that, and said he would give our conditions some thought before getting in touch again.'

'Quick thinker.' Connie, smiling now, held out a thick manila envelope secured with brass-tagged red laces. Inside was Buckingham Palace accreditation for Mr. John Birton, photo-journalist, Rapix Worldwide Syndication, 5c Chancery Lane, London, E.C.4.

Birton fingered the engraved coat of arms on the accreditation. Back in the sun again—the richest hunt in the world—the hunt for the jackpot shot that needed no caption yet told it all.

Di with the kid on her hip, and the sun shining through her dress, outlining those legs. Or the high-angle boob-shot of her in the black velvet number.

Connie's thoughts ran with his. He was thinking pix. So was she. Before leaving, he'd mentioned the pic he'd taken of D'Acre caught between Di and Charlie. Connie said:

'You didn't tell me how you got the magic pic.'

'Easy, darling. There I was in a mad scrum. French photogs there.

The maddest. Jerries, too. I stuck the 35 on motor-drive and held it up. Perfect shot. Rex D'Acre between Di and Charlie. Hole in the paper, so it got a run. Know something? Poor old D'Acre, he's still caught between them. I reckon he thinks he can bring them together again.'

'Togetherness, love it.' Connie said, moving from the office area to the studio.

Birton followed her.

Back in the hunt.

But not just one of the boozy pack he had inside running.

– 18 –

Albany, London, S.W.1

Guy Jessop slammed the phone down: his fifth call to Milan. Dusé, the ex-Bersagliere, must be on one of his government assignments. Which government? The elected one? Or the unelected—otherwise known as the Mafia?

For a mad instant, Jessop toyed with the notion of taking on the D'Acre task himself. Yet much as he might relish the thought of knocking over a clutch of journalists, he knew his marksmanship wasn't five-slash-one-thousand class. He'd been squad buffoon in musketry. Alisdair Guthrie had been *Numero Uno*. Pity he wasn't available.

Missing in action. What a way to go—maintaining the silliest bloody border bar none in a world of silly bloody borders.

Jessop surveyed his drawing-room, its gilt-framed paintings, its plump, shining furniture, its flowers, Emma's touch. There was the true rub. Not musketry. Emma. She was shopping at what she liked to call the 'corner store'—Fortnum and Mason. She wouldn't be best pleased if he got directly involved and something went wrong to disturb her shopping. As it was, she was inclined to ask questions about his Kaleidoscope agency that were slightly too pertinent.

He gulped a mouthful of pink gin. 'Neutralising the social infrastructure'. No doubt about it, Americans had a definite gift for humbug. In fact, their humbug was like their dry Martinis, long on insane gin, short on sweet reason. It was as if composing their

Declaration of Independence had exhausted their capacity for plain speech. No, even there, they were already into humbug. '... Life, Liberty and the pursuit of happiness ...' How could you pursue happiness? They meant money.

The Almighty Greenback.

Pursuit of happiness humbug. Like, 'neutralising the social infrastructure'.

Quaint way to describe assassination: Operation Phoenix.

He moved to the window and looked into Albany's darkening interior courtyard. Green, country quiet yet only a stoned stumble from Piccadilly. Observer, attached to an American Sea Air Land team on Phoenix duty in the Mekong delta. Subsequently, he'd been posted to S.A.S. HQ, Swanbourne Barracks, Perth.

'Pink Un'. They'd nicknamed him, the Aussies: 'Pink 'Un, the Pom', lying on the ocean beach against which the barracks were backed. Huge blue skies. Rolling swells. And the most astounding women.

The Killing House, dim, acrid with cordite and deadly lead dust from automatic weapons fired on close-combat simulations designed to impress 'Pink 'Un, the Pom, the observer. And he had observed their instant intensity, cool ferocity and lethal swiftness.

The Killing House and the HQ legend: the Officers Mess regaining control of the unit from the Sergeants Mess back in the Seventies. Not exactly a decimation of non-coms. But enough.

One of them: Garbo. Gave him his edge. No one harder than a sergeant pissed off about being made to piss off. Something else. Something even harder.

As Jessop had observed later when he'd met Garbo working on short-term contract for the Hong Kong police anti-drug squad.

Tungsten on steel.

Totally undeflectable.

'No.' Jessop said the word aloud to reinforce its impact. He couldn't—wouldn't—mustn't—break his rule against casting a specialist on successive gigs.

But D'Acre'd nominated a theatre and a date.

None more dramatic, if you had journalists on a headliner bill.

Jessop reached for the telephone and tapped in Garbo's mobile number. He let it ring three times before switching off. After five seconds, he rang again and got no further than identifying himself. 'Rack off, Pink 'Un,' Garbo said. 'You're a balls-up artist and you still owe me, you bastard.'

When Jessop rang again, a recorded voice informed him that the mobile phone was switched off.

He thought of re-trying Dusé, the Olympian Bersagliere. Forget Dusé.

Bernhardt, a better bet.

Jessop tapped in a Tel Aviv number. He went through his contact drill again.

'You don't give people much time to respond.'

Emma.

She'd been shopping. Something more delicious than Fortnum and Mason groceries. A wine-coloured silk kimono which, when she pirouetted, he saw was embroidered with pink-cherry blossom. How could anyone so small fill his vision?

The telephone shrilled and Bernhardt's growl filled his ear. 'One minute,' Jessop said and covered the telephone with his hand to speak to Emma. She, however, had taken the remark to herself. 'Thirty seconds,' she said, already withdrawing. 'Or I'll change into my recycled carpet slippers.'

His name for the Winceyette nightdresses, she sometimes wore. Jessop fell to his knees, shaking his head to her threat, and nodding to her time limit. His conversation with Bernhardt took longer but it was positive. Bernhardt was resting between shows and would be available for a headliner spot on November 14. Usual terms.

'Lovely theatre,' Jessop said.

'Long or short engagement?'

'Long.' Jessop meant rifle.

'Any support act?'

'No, you're solo. But there's a trio involved. They'll be marked for you when you get there. I'd allow a week for rehearsals.'

'Ten days. It could be fatal to go on under-rehearsed.'

'True. What about props? Need any help?'

'No. It will be more diplomatic—you understand?—if I use my own method. The fee, I pick up going in, coming out.'

Jessop understood. Bernhardt travelled under diplomatic cover with his props—rifle and ammunition—safe from search in a diplomatic bag.

'Ireland's your first stop,' Jessop said. 'Contact me from there and I'll give you the theatre, date and time.'

'Shalom.'

Peace was not exactly predominant in Emma's demeanour. She was wearing her thickest Winceyette nightdress. Jessop had guessed as much and brought an antidote: two flutes and a bottle of Bollinger.

'Urgent call obviously,' she said.

'Showbiz types. You know how they are—all facade and fragile egos. When they need to talk to you, it's absolutely now, luvey.'

'What about me?'

'You're absolutely now, too.' He was attempting the difficult trick of unwiring and peeling the foil off the champagne bottle while trying to unpeel the Winceyette. 'You know I think your Pope should ban these garments instead of French letters.'

A mistake. She had a thing about the Pope. 'When was the last time you took gutshots for what you believed?'

'Not recently.' He fingered his scar-puckered eye to remind her that he had been at the sharp end. She took the glass of champagne he offered, clinked glasses and sipped before peeling off the recycled carpet slippers. Four more points to him, not the winning point.

When he lay beside her, she patted his belly. 'I want one of those.'

Jessop was by no means dim. It took him only half a glass of champagne to realise what she meant. 'You've already been pregnant. Twice.' he said. 'Or have you—neglectful mummy—forgotten your sons Eric and Rufus even now dreaming of you on the cold water-beds of Gordonstoun.'

'Daughter. And I want one now.'

'Impossible.'

'As soon as possible then.'

'Out of the question.'

'You told me, your vasectomy, you told me it was the reversible kind.'

'It is.'

'No problem.'

'A daughter.'

'Maybe two.'

'Two? You may not even get one. You may get another son.'

'That would please you After all, you wouldn't have had the vasectomy—or did it have you?—if you hadn't already had your sons.'

'I did it for you.'

'Oh, please, you'll be telling me in a moment you did it to save a whale. You did it for bonking anonymous. Now get it reversed.'

Her tone made it clear to Jessop that there was something more impermeable to his sexual charisma than recycled carpet-slippers: Emma's determination.

– 19 –

Loch Fyneside, Argyll

Garbo plunged his dirk into the warm belly of the beast and ripped it open. Wind-driven sleet pattered on his hooded, dark-green poncho and scoured blood from his hands as he scooped out the beast's stomach, heavy with partly digested grass, and then the liver, lights and heart.

No way the L42A1 wasn't zeroed in. The ripped heart told it all. Tricky shot: the light going, the beast startled, quartering away from him with its hinds for some reason. Yet he'd heart-nailed it at seven-fifty. One shot. Not bad after the uphill approach-march into the wind and the final stalk.

Downhill to his front, a burn roared in spate and foamed over a rocky ledge to plunge into a pool. Beside the pool, the tumbled stone walls of an ancient house. He cut the beast's leg tendons and began sawing at its neck, gripping its antlers to steady the head. At least twelve points. A royal?

'No more hundred-and-fifty a carcass for you, pal.'

What the remark meant. Garbo wasn't sure. He didn't need to know. The tone of the voice was enough. And he realised what had startled the beast. While he'd been stalking it, he himself had been stalked.

Gamekeeper.

Garbo slashed the last sinew on the beast's neck to sever the head from the body. 'Slowly, man. Dirk down and turn slowly.' Garbo obeyed, except that he didn't turn all that slowly. As he did, he swung the beast's head by one of his antlers. The gamekeeper got off a single shot which thudded into the beast's head. He did not get off another. Garbo was on him.

Stupid bastard. Didn't have enough sense to stand off at least ten paces when bailing up an enemy. Again and again, Garbo rammed the points of the beast's antlers into the gamekeeper's chest, face, throat. It was the throat wound that did for him, his life's blood jetting from his jugular onto Garbo who raised his face to the scouring sleet.

He put his boot to the body of the beast and pushed. It half rolled, half-slithered down the slope towards the burn. He went after it, dragging it by its foreleg towards the pool. From the ruined house, he took a squared off stone and rammed it into the beast's belly cavity. And another. Then he heaved the body into the pool. It sank leaving no trace.

He searched the ruin. On the floor was a rusting wire bedspring, its wooden frame rotted. He pulled the spring clear and clambered up the slope with it. At the pool's edge, he rolled the stag's head in the spring, securing its ends by jamming them over the antler tines. Into the pool it splashed to join the body. Back up the hill, he went.

The lightning flashed. The thunder rolled as if the mountains were tumbling down. From the body of the dead gamekeeper a two-way radio beeped like a bird. Contact call. Base? Or a partner out here on the killing ground? Garbo found his dirk and sheathed it along his leg. From under the rock shelf where he'd stowed it, he retrieved the L424A1 and slung it muzzle down under his poncho. The gamekeeper had come at him from the west. Any partner would be moving in from the east.

Pincer movement.

Go.

North.

Garbo was already moving on the thought, moving below the skyline, moving fast. But not far. In the lea of a bush, he took off his boots and socks. From the side pocket of his combat strides, he took a plastic bag holding a pair of dry socks and a hand towel. He dried his feet and put on the fresh socks. A lace broke as he tied his second boot. Shit but no disaster. He always carried a spare pair.

He moved again. Still heading north but faster. There were towns within striking distance. Villages, too. The name Rest and Be Thankful mocked his rush through the storm which had returned the terrain to its primeval state, awaiting its first incomers to seed themselves and grow their mighty tree of clan and gens. He found one of their paths, winding among hummocks of heather, light rustling stands of birch and rowan, dark, silent blotches of fir.

Off to his left, a bird cried. Curlew? From his right came a matching response. Within heartbeats, he was in a rousing, flaring encampment of ghosts, realising that the curlew cries had been outpost signals, realising that the ghosts were all too solid.

Tinkers?

But tinkers would never be so far off main roads and without vehicles or caravans. They were screaming and shouting at him, women and men, girls and boys, in a mix of dialect, barely understood, and what he took to be Gaelic which he did not understand at all.

One fronted him. Big guy, black-bearded, wild-eyed, wilder hair crowned with a bonnet from which sprouted a bedraggled eagle feather. Big guy with a big dog. The wildest. Deerhound. But heavy in the head. Squat. Maybe a touch of Rottweiler, beloved symbol of apartheid. Well trained. Not a growl out of it, sitting waiting for the attack command from the big guy. 'McAdam Mhor,' he said. 'And who might you be?'

'Lost,' Garbo said. 'I'm lost.'

‘Lost, is it? How can that be, and you on the best-known ground of all the world that belongs to me and mine.’

‘The storm caught me on the hill.’

‘Aye, but for what purpose were you on the hill. Not hiking, I’ll be bound.’ He flicked Garbo’s poncho to one side to reveal the L42A1. ‘That’s no cromach you’re carrying.’

McAdam Mhor’s speech matched his garb: a hairy tartan blanket, kilted and belted round his waist with the end thrown over his shoulder. To his side came a supple slip of a woman, all hungry eyes, hollow cheeks and feral red hair, garbed like him except that her blanket was skirted and carried up and over her breasts. So were they all dressed. No firearms. A couple of bows. A crossbow. The men all carried claymores and dirks.

Wild, oh, wild in the lights that’d flared when he blundered among them yet somehow artificial like McAdam Mhor who may have preferred the dog to the woman for he fondled its ears with never a glance at her. ‘Stick from the forest, fish from the river, deer from the hill,’ he was saying. ‘Our ancient way. But not without the chieftain’s yea. And I’m the very chieftain.’

An approving cheer greeted this, growing louder as he went on. ‘McAdam, son of McAdam and all the Adams since old, sweating time began in the kenning of the first Adam and his Eve.’

Video-camera.

A follower had one focused on McAdam Mhor and he was playing to it. ‘No man comes armed onto my ground without paying a forfeit.’ Not a ghost. The leader of a group, haunted by the past and trying to regain it from the kind of present that involved cardboard cottages. ‘Tell me this and tell me no more. How much would that bit of gun be worth to you?’

Garbo unslung the L42A1 and gave it to McAdam Mhor—butt to

jaw and felt both butt and jaw give as McAdam Mhor went down, and his dog rose, snarling, only to be silenced and knocked sprawling over its master by the impact of the 7.62 round Garbo fired at its head. He leapt over them to run from the flaring time-warp into the darkness beyond.

Shrieks and howls followed him and an arrow hissed past him. It was the crossbow he feared. He'd used one. All he needed was a four-barbed crossbow bolt in his back. He turned and fired five rounds rapid over the heads of his immediate pursuers.

They went to ground. Only the supple slip of a woman with the feral red hair came on. 'Take me,' she said. 'Take me with you.'

'I don't know where I'm going.'

'No more do I.'

Mad.

Not as mad as those who lived in cardboard cottages, swilling meths and worse when they could be making Molotov cocktails to singe the arses off their silvertail exploiters.

'Sorry.' Garbo turned from her. Yet the image of her face, her eyes, her hair went before him so strongly that he was able to persuade himself that she and her clan were no more than a fantasy brought on by the sick exhilaration of the kill.

North ten Ks, Garbo jogged, swung east and downhill to where he'd cached the Zodiac on Loch Fyne shore below Inverary. He did not use the outboard. He rowed down-loch, the L41A1 back in the guitar and its case, a fishing line streamed from the stern: hippie fisherman after a bad night.

Bloody bad.

One gamekeeper gored to death by a wild beast.

One fantasy chieftain with a broken jaw.

One hound dead.

– 20 –

Rotten Row, Hyde Park, W.1

Dawn mist, early birds on the wing, on foot and on horseback, Rex D'Acre one of them, all grey like his horse, so both looked as if they might have been sculpted from the mist. D'Acre was managing the horse—a gelding—with determined competence, and dismounted in similar fashion when—surprise! surprise!—he saw Birton. 'What brings you here so early?'

Birton had done his share of meets with punters trying to add melodrama to the business of selling their lives at so many pix and words per pound, 'Got your call, didn't I?'

'A moment.' D'Acre was going through the motions of tightening the saddle girth.

The gelding was reacting as if he were taking its inside leg measurement to fit it with trousers. Birton, who'd worked with horses when he could still think he would be forever small enough to be a jockey, held the gelding's head soothingly.

D'Acre handed him a black cap buttoned red on top and badged in front with a red crown. 'Congratulations. You've been chosen-to wear this. Experiment, and for that reason discreet. But you may find wearing it on royal assignments leads to your being singled out for special treatment.'

'I see.'

Birton thought he did. He knew, as only a pro could, that the royals not only played to the cameras, they played better to some cameras than to others: the straight into the lens smile that made the difference between an intimate shot and a snatched one. He hadn't been particularly favoured. Now things would be different.

He was more than happy to give D'Acre a boost when it came to re-mounting and got off a shot of him riding back in the direction of the Household Cavalry barracks, his parting words lingering. 'You'll get our call soon. Location. Date.'

Our.

Soon.

Location.

Date.

– 21 –

Rapix Studio, Chancery Lane, E.C.4.

Reconciliation. It had to be: a secret reconciliation between Charlie and Di. Balmoral? No, Craigowen Lodge, Charlie's favourite hideaway. Exclusive series of pix for worldwide syndication. Charlie and Di hand-in-hand. Looking at each other. Kissing and making up. Perfect.

Or what about that Hebridean island where Charlie liked to play crofter prince during the polo off-season? Berneray, that was it.

Except Di was a sun bug. That spot in the Kalahari Desert where Charlie went with Laurens van der Post—Deception Pan?

No, wrong kind of name.

Taj Mahal. The thought excited Birton so much that he repeated it aloud and Connie Gaudren gasped: 'Curry. How can you think of curry now?' Birton wasn't thinking curry, he was thinking of the Taj Mahal by moonlight: the Charlie-Di gig to India in '91 when she decided to have herself snapped sitting alone on a marble bench in front of the mausoleum Shah Jehan had built as a last resting place for his wife Mumtaz and himself, the place Charlie promised to take Di.

Shit, twelve years ago.

Now Charlie boy was going to make good his promise. Birton framed the shot in his mind. The two most famous profiles in the world caught in silhouette as their heads inclined for a kiss against the arches and the Taj Mahal dome, timeless symbol of married love.

All right. All right. The old Shah Jehan had other wives beside Mumtaz. But she was his favourite. No question. And that would feed to the story: Di had to be Charlie's favourite in the end. Birton knew. He'd snapped the pick of the other runners: Di's sister Sarah, Davina Sheffield, Lady Jane Wellesley, Amanda Knatchbull, Anna Wallace and Sabrina Guinness. Camilla Parker-Bowles? You've got to be joking. Di was the pick of the pick.

Standing on the end of the studio four-poster, Connie Gaudren cocked the red and black cap over her right eye and struck a pose that mixed satire, provocation and—it couldn't be but it was—love. 'Suits me better than you.' Lying back in the four-poster, his Nikon to his eye, Jack Birton did not disagree as Connie to the rhythm of her blood and the metronome click of the camera proceeded through a series of poses, using the baseball cap to cover her breasts in turn, her quim and, in a giggling reflex of modesty, her face.

'On your head,' he said. 'Centred. I want to get the crown full on.' Connie did as instructed.

'Beaut-i-ful,' he said, knocking off three shots.

How lucky could a guy get? A temp who came to type and stayed to dot more than his Is and cross more than his Ts. Long live the European Community when it meant Anglo-French-Tahitian temps.

'Things are going to be different,' he said.

'I'm enjoying them as they are.'

Things would be different. D'Acre had given him a hint on an extraordinary royal photo-opportunity. 'Remember the photograph of His Royal Highness kissing Her Royal Highness after their wedding?'

How could Birton forget that Charlie and Di shot? Like the first kiss of two shy lovers in the back balcony of the local fleapit—except that it was on the front balcony of Buckingham Palace with thousands cheering and millions watching on the telly.

There he was Numero Stinko, battling to hold on to his job after the cock-up pic. He'd hustled from St Paul's to the palace and set up his step-ladder in a heaving ocean of bodies.

Talk about Humpty-bleeding-Dumpty.

And where was his bleeding wordsman: Roger the Dodger Delamere? Getting vox pops in the crowd, that's where instead of holding the ladder steady.

One shot. One shot before he came tumbling down. But not the jackpot shot.

Not the kiss.

Enraptured now by Connie's, Birton put the Nikon down to hold her.

Charlie and Di. Close shot? Long shot? He'd need the big artillery. Six hundred, 1200. Wide-angle might be an idea as well. Create a sense of love in a goldfish bowl.

With the loot, he'd be able to get his Barbican flat back and set up a sunny winter base. France. Spain. Connie needed the sun. Her skin, the gold of it, took on a kind of tarnish in the London winter.

– 22 –

Saint James's Palace, London W.1

From the mullioned window of his tower room, Rex D'Acre peered into the rain-swept courtyard where His Royal Highness Prince Charles in green Barbour jacket and grey-green Balmoral tweed ratting cap was ducking into his Aston Martin, his close protection officer, Detective Superintendent Colin Trimming in attendance.

Off to the country, and Highgrove. Absolutely no doubt—though problematical whether H.R.H. would confine himself to intercourse with the Highgrove flowers or permit himself equivalent intimacies with his forget-me-not, Camilla Parker-Bowles, at neighbouring Middlewick House.

D'Acre returned to his desk. He'd retained the duty of maintaining the master log. He pulled it to him and picked up the telephone to complete the round of calls.

Clarence House, and the Queen Mother's staff. Tincture of regret there. He' d been made aware he would be welcome to join her household. Best food and wine in the royal circle. Brightest wit. The Queen Mother, having telephoned her butler's pantry and been kept waiting by chatterbox servants: 'I don't know about you old queens but this old Queen wants a drink.'

Such chiffon vim. Such pastel vigour.

An impresario to whose plays D'Acre sometimes played angel had unsuccessfully sought his investment in a production of the Scottish play in which Macbeth was to be a stutterer in moments of crisis and his wife douce-seeming yet ruthless: 'Infirm of purpose, give me the daggers.'

The Queen Mother had certainly cut the Duke of Windsor down to size and with him the bride he'd preferred to her, Wallis Simpson.

The Royal Ghetto: Kensington Palace. The staffs of H.R.H. Princess Margaret and 'Our Val'—short for Valkyrie—the Queen's nickname for Princess Michael of Kent which presumably made her husband some kind of Odin.

D'Acre regarded the silver-framed photograph of himself with Prince Charles and Princess Diana. Lucky snapshot. Both had made overtures. Not directly, of course. That was not the way things were done. He'd been to Kensington Palace, and seen her beauty blaze from the garden, heard her voice change from svelte charm to childish tantrum.

And been reminded of the only woman he'd ever come near to loving: how she would lie on the floor—soignée, sophisticated—and in a trice become a child wild for her own way, drumming her heels upon the floor as if she were back in the nursery and he were her nanny to be terrorised into compliance: scarcely the kind of woman to share a grace-and-favour residence.

It was with a sense of pleasure that he made his call to the staff of Princess Diana. He duly entered the details in the master log under those he had already made about H.R.H. the Queen, H.R.H. Prince Philip, H.R.H. Princess Anne, H.R.H. Prince Andrew and H.R.H. Prince Edward and other lesser royals. He'd recently added to the information he collated, details of clothes, jewellery and decorations to be worn, a service much appreciated by the distaff royals.

He'd allowed himself a variant on his habit of using fountain pens. He sometimes used a black swan quill. Not wholly traditional for it had a calligrapher's gold nib. He'd been conscious of H.R.H., observing this. A minor eccentricity went some way to separating one from the ruck. Not that there was much of a ruck. Nonethless, he was low man on the totem pole.

For the time being.

He turned to completing a draft analysis of the Prince's Trust, set up in 1976, his black quill pen scratching over the white parchment-finish paper, the soft light cast by a brass, green-shaded lamp, carrying him back through the continuities of the palace: the king who'd built the palace: Henry VIII; the stay of Charles I on the night before his execution, the births there of Charles II and George IV.

D'Acre shivered, not so much because of the lack of heat from the one-bar electric fire enjoined by royal frugality as momentarily fearful of being Tudor in a Tudor palace, engaged in a Tudor plot on which the future of the monarchy might well depend as much as it had the other plots enacted within the red brick walls of Saint James.

Writing finished, he sat with his eyes shut. His tower room was close enough to the clock on the palace façade to hear its cogs and levers ticking—creaking—with the weight of the centuries. He kept his eyes closed until the clock struck the hours: five. He then read the Conclusion to his analysis.

'The Prince's Trust has a total income of £30 million a year from its spread of charitable projects. It has funded 17,500 small businesses, two thirds of which are viable.

'What next?

'Another question, perhaps: "To be or not to be?" This may have had ultimate relevance for the Prince of Denmark. It does not necessarily have similar relevance for the Prince of Wales, facing not only, "the slings and arrows of outrageous fortune" but the even more outrageous clichés of hireling Scribes and Pharisees.

‘Rather the relevant question is: To be or to do? The answer thereto is a paradox: the modern prince must be and do. Given this, and given that a significant number of Prince’s Trust enterprises have gone beyond viability to attain critical mass, it may be opportune to consider the possibility of making such enterprises subsidiaries of mainstream companies, thus exploiting the potential synergies between the Prince’s Trust and companies controlled by members of another organisation under princely patronage: the Business Leaders Forum.

‘This linkage would create a base for a pre-emptive claim to more than merely royal patronage; that is, the administration of the Millennium Fund to mark the next thousand years, beginning January 1, 2001 (projected revenue from a one-fifth share of the National Lottery: £1 billion).

‘Revenue of this order of magnitude under royal patronage and royal administration would surely conduce to being and doing in a manner to add authority to what Walter Bagheot saw as the Monarch’s role: “Being consulted, encouraging and warning”.’

A loyal Conclusion.

With a loyal operation in train.

– 23 –

International Hotel, Bray, Ireland

Michael MacLirr, despite the fine cut of his Donegal tweeds, was no gentleman, one reason why he did not prefer the blonde in black sitting opposite him in the long bar overlooking the grey wash of the Irish Sea, rendered all-encompassing by the grey fall of rain in the soft afternoon light.

Alice Anne Johnson, he thought. A gravestone name for a phony passport if ever there was one. 'Would you listen, really listen, woman, listen for a second?' His Ulster hammer-on-anvil vowels were pitched below the ambient music, jazzman Ben Webster's version of, *The Londonderry Air,* a nice distraction for any Brit or Gardai Special Branch bugger. 'Would you listen, I say, for even half a second for that's all the wit you have about you.'

She turned the blank of her shades on him. 'I have listened. And for more than a second. So far what I've heard is you made a bloody muck of a simple exercise, the leads you had.'

'Haven't I told you frontwards and backwards, we couldn't use the leads obviously? Will I tell you again, sideways, the why of it?' A waiter hovered: bold stamp of a young fella, a bowtie on him that might light up or spin. He was moving in.

MacLirr waved him off: fist. Christ Almighty in his glory: his own minder moving in to protect him from this woman. He must seem like a honeymooner losing the first round on points. A private room would've been better, except he had a thing about private rooms since that Hush Puppy team almost lifted him when he was sniffing round the Royal Cork Yacht Club for a handy boat.

Cute Sassies. None cuter. Stake-out where a man would go who had guns to run.

'Straight,' she was saying. 'Just tell me straight.' And her sipping on the champagne cocktail he'd bought her, daft at the sight of her swaying walk.

'You must see,' he said. 'You must, using the leads might've compromised you.'

She scratched her blonde hair. 'How—and him in close custody?'

'The Maze is close custody. But men escape. He could've—or been rescued. Nearly was. Don't you see, if we'd been making a big thing of the leads, where would you have been? Not sitting here large as life and twice as blonde like Marilyn Monroe, poor bitch, wondering which of the Kennedys was going to bed her next.'

'Don't talk like that.'

He was drinking iced water. 'Add some soap to this and you can wash my mouth out.' He proffered his glass. 'Go on, sister.'

She swept her own glass in an arc towards him. He jerked back but her cocktail drenched his face and dripped onto his fine raiment. Her voice was low and cutting for his balls. 'You dare sermonise me. That remark, if I were to report it, your recent promotion would be the height of your fall.'

Honeymoon, he was thinking as he dried himself with his handkerchief. We're into the marriage, and I'm losing on points there as well. He glanced round the bar. The other drinkers were having a great time pretending not to notice. Who said karaoke had killed floorshows?

'All right,' he said. 'The leads, the ruffian leads were good leads, sure enough.' He waved his handkerchief dismissively. 'But someone wanting journalists duffed up?'

'Not someone, someone from Buckingham Palace: Rex D'Acre.'

'My memory's fine, woman. I also remember Guy Jessop turned the job down—denied being into *keeni-meeni*. What a hoot. Too tricky even for him, a loony from Loonybin Palace involved. And bottom line: it didn't affect our ground directly, did it?'

'Jessop's a liar, and hire killing's his thing. Us. And worse.'

'I know. I know. The Jessop ploy—waste others. Blame us. But you're not suggesting he's taken the job, that he's got one of his killing's on?'

'That's what you were supposed to establish—you who's now All Ireland Intelligence Co-ordinator for the Army Council.' She pushed her chair away from the table. 'I'll find out myself. That place leaks like a sieve.'

'You're not going back.'

'I'm booked return through Schipol. Expected tomorrow.'

'Expected maybe. But it might be a colder welcome than you bargained for. You're under investigation.'

'Impossible. She was watching his eyes. He wasn't bluffing. 'How?'

'Standard procedure. Backtrack. You said yourself the sieve. Everyone knew about you and the Jock.'

'Guthrie. Alisdair Guthrie. Major Alisdair Guthrie.'

'The very same. They'll lift you for questioning sooner or later, and later or sooner, discover what you've been doing.' He baited her. 'Sister.'

One rise was all he was going to get out of her. From his jacket pocket he took a hotel tagged key. 'There's a room booked for you here. I'll take you up.'

'Only if I have your word—our ruffian—a whiff of anyone like him and you tell me.'

'Frontwards, backwards, sideways, straight. Or didn't I tell you,' he said. 'You're under my command. The wind from London—Englishman he speak with forked fart—the wind from London's changing, and you've been assigned to help me read it.'

Carrying his icewater, he shepherded her towards her room, hoping the weight and the height he had on her might give his minder an impression of dominance. But there was no dominating this woman. 'You'll tell me,' she said. 'Right away.'

'If I do hear, and I think it concerns you.'

'Oh, it concerns me. I feel I have widow's rights on it.'

'Widow's rights, is it?'

'Betrayer's rights, then—and they're as strong as yours.' Stronger she thought. For she had misjudged her man, thinking he would talk as easily under torture as he'd talked under her.

'Mine?' MacLirr was saying.

'Torturer's rights,' she said. 'Executioner's rights.'

'Big boys' games, big boys' rules.'

He watched her go. A mistake to tell her about that. She'd weaseled it out of him. Still maybe he shouldn't've recalled the Jock's prayer. Nor his last words.

At the doorway of her room, she repeated them: 'Sir Jesus, forgive us all.'

She scratched her blonde hair. 'I hate this. Absolutely hate it, like wearing a pup with fleas.' She pulled it off. Beneath it her own hair lay coiled. She shook it free and it shivered red to her shoulders: Pamela Fitzgibbon. And slammed the door in his face.

The spirit of her. The voice of her. The face of her. The swaying walk of her. What wouldn't the medianiks give for her story?

Half a million? And the rest. Could they protect the informer? Devil the bit of it. Like terrs themselves, medianiks. Hearts for it—if not the guts. Move in on lives—slash, burn, publish, profit and be damned.

There were others—MI5, M16—more reliable than medianiks who might relish a quiet meeting, or two, with the elegant Pamela Fitzgibbon.

Aristo descendant of a demon of Irish politics, educated by Benedictine nuns at the posh Kylemore Abbey, Connemara who thought she, too, might become a nun. Which was why he could get a rise out of her by calling her sister.

All the right connections for Buckingham Palace, the same woman. Inspired, so she said, to work for the I.R.A. by the death of hunger striker Bobby Sands and the need to right the wrongs set in train by her ancestor.

The Army Council had loved it. Besotted with her, the idea of having someone inside Loonybin Palace.

But was her say-so true? That was the beauty of his thinking. If she were a Brit double agent, as he suspected, MI5 or MI6 wouldn't be too keen. If she were truly I.R.A, the same pishrogues would pay handsomely.

Plus plusses: indemnity against prosecution for past crimes against the Crown.

New identity.

New life over the hills—aye and the seas—and faraway.

And the second option didn't necessarily make a dud cheque of the first. Maybe get MI5 and M16 into a bidding war. Tie that up. Then a deal with the merry medianiks.

Have to lift her. The price would be higher for delivery. Odds Judas was offered twenty pieces of silver for location: Garden of Gesthsemene. Thirty pieces for a recognition sign: a kiss. What would he've got had he been game to lift his man away from the likes of Peter and his sword? Fifty pieces.

MacLirr finished his iced water. With this thinking, he might have to get back to sobering whiskey. His minder was looking at his watch. MacLirr looked at his own Rolex Perpetual: 4 pm.

And the cock crowing.

– 24 –

Grand East, Duke Street, S.W.1

Rex D'Acre came down the stairs from the stately interior of freemasonry's most prestigious meeting place with its Red Room, Black Room and Chamber of Death.

Haunting music to match his mood resounded in his mind: Mozart's music for *The Magic Flute.* In D'Acre's mind, the music accompanied other words: Knight of the Pelican and Eagle and Sovereign Prince Rose Croix of Heredom.

Death and resurrection.

The mimed death and resurrection of the body, central to exaltation into the Eighteenth Degree of the Ancient and Accepted Rite of Holy Royal Arch.

More.

He had been exalted to the seventeen other degrees of Royal Arch leading to Rose Croix.

The music shifted: Secret Master, Perfect Master, Intimate Secretary, Provost and Judge Intendant of the Building, Elect of Nine, Elect of Fifteen, Sublime Elect, Grand Master Elect, Royal Arch of Enoch, Scottish Knight of Perfection, Knight of the Sword, Prince of Jerusalem and Knight of the East and West.,

Never had D'Acre felt such a sense of destiny.

Exaltation.

Exultation.

Ecstasy.

Yes, ecstasy in yet other degrees to which he aspired: Grand Inspector Inquisitor—400 members only—Sublime Prince of the Royal Secret—180 members—and Grand Inspector General—75 members.

Sublime Prince of the Royal Secret.

The profane were to an extent correct, D'Acre thought, as the music soared. The Blue Lodge degrees—Entered Apprentice, Fellow Craft and Master Mason—were soap opera compared to the grand opera of the Red, the Royal Arch, degrees.

Ammi Ruhamah, the password to supreme degrees, Ammi Ruhamah—My people have found mercy—was worthy of an aria.

Mozart's music was still with D'Acre as he exited through a first double door. As he came to a second, a voice rapped, as sharply as a conductor's baton on a music stand: 'Congratulations.'

D'Acre had been more surprised to see Guy Jessop taking part in the rituals than Jessop had been to see D'Acre as a candidate. Jessop knew the importance of a suitable work address when it came to admission to Royal Arch. The Palace of Saint James was one of the best.

Together they walked up Duke Street, D'Acre in a dark overcoat with bowler hat. Jessop in a trilby and British warm. His father's coat but not worn by him because he'd not made the commissioned rank to which he aspired. Warrant Officer First Class was his limit in the Army. But not in Freemasonry.

'We're very convenient here.' Jessop spoke as if Grand East were simply another club like nearby White's or Boodles. 'Locks, purveyor of hats, Lobb's of shoes, Turnbull and Asser of shirts, with all the tailors of Savile Row waiting to charge serious sums of money to correct the hump on your back as they tried to do for Richard Third.' Without changing his bantering tone, he went on: 'Talking of purveyors to the gentry, the number I gave you.'

'Most helpful,' D'Acre said. 'Agenda One, forgive my mentioning it ...'

Stark, raving bonkers, as who was it said? Jessop had seen it in his father, the Warrant Officer First Class. Resentment at the distinction between warrants and commissions. The relish in masonic superiority over commissioned officers. His father'd collected lodges like stamps, valuable stamps, that had given Jessop entry to the Royal Masonic School for Boys, Eton enough for a commission.

'Delighted,' he said. 'Delighted you mentioned it. Was about to myself. Agenda One is mainly a military lodge as you might imagine. We work Knights Templar ritual. Swords. Surcoats. Chainmail. But fear not, civilian members are not completely unknown. In any case, wouldn't do for us to be more picky than Rose Croix about a distinguished royal household member. They had reached Piccadilly. Jessop gestured left towards the Ritz. 'I'm having a drink, incredibly my wife Emma. Don't suppose you'd care to join us?'

D'Acre who understood Jessop's kind of English perfectly said: 'Must rush. Appointment I'm afraid.'

Jessop smiled as he watched D'Acre walk towards Piccadilly Circus and its statue of Eros. Janus, he thought. Should be the statue of Janus. This is a two-faced city. Or is that three?

He was still smiling when he met his wife in the Ritz bar. Like many women confident of her beauty, she had no inhibitions about clichés. She wore a mink coat draped on her shoulders, a little black dress and pearls and said: 'You look like the cat who swallowed the canary.'

Jessop smiled more broadly, his scarred eye squinching up. 'Not the canary. Possibly a pigeon—cock pigeon.'

'You are being cryptic. I do hope you mean the operation has been a success.'

'Looking good,' Jessop said. 'What did you say you wanted? Little blonde or little brunette?'

'A little Gordon's and Dubonnet—before I swear off.'

'Very good, m'lady.'

'And you can think about swearing off yourself.'

At the Rapix Studios Rex D'Acre didn't feel disposed to have a long conversation with the creep hound Jack Birton. Nor did Birton, wearing a rusty black silk dressing gown that Noel Coward might've donated to charity half-a-century before.

Nevertheless D'Acre's information delighted him, the information on location and time. Remembering his manners—or possibly haunted by the ghost of the dressing gown—Birton said: 'Care for a spot of something?'

'Another time. My cab's waiting.'

Exalted and exultant.

Sublime Prince of the Royal Secret.

As such prepared to admit there were honourable Free Masons who'd think he was off the square in his gross abuse of the Craft and would expel him if they found out. But what was the point of a secret society if it could not use its secrecy secretly.

– 25 –

Golden Square, London, W.1

Guy Jessop never panicked. 'It's all adrenalin,' he would say. 'You decide whether to use it for fight or flight.'

Nonetheless he wasn't exactly buoyant about the paragraph in *Comic Cuts,* as he called *The Sun:*

> TUBE DEATH
> 'A man, identified as Luther Stone,
> an American in transit from Israel,
> fell in front of a train at Heathrow
> Underground Station yesterday.
> Police said there appeared to
> be no suspicious circumstances.'

Well, Jessop thought, he certainly wouldn't be identified by his real name: Aaron Levi. Nor would there be any suspicious circumstances. That was the point. But accidents didn't happen to chaps who'd contrived so many accidents for others. He'd been knocked off.

Jessop picked up his copy of *The Times* and put it down again. No point in cross-checking. Aaron Levi, alias Bernhardt, and more other work names than you could shake a Torah at, wasn't going to rate an obituary although in his field he'd been something of an artist.

No shortage of enemies. Even his friends might not, be completely delighted if they'd learned he was on moonlight contracts.

Deadline contracts.

Jessop rubbed his scarred eye. He had the number of subjects. He had the location and date. He had the markers. He had the upfront fee plus expenses ready and waiting. The black attaché case containing it stood end up on his desk.

A tombstone to Bernhardt. He raised a glass of pink gin. 'Shalom'.

Dusé, the ex-Bersagliere, he'd tried again as soon as he read the news of Bernhardt's death. No go.

He had one more headliner: Dietrich.

Last known address: Sarajevo.

– 26 –

Ocean Drummer, Loch Fyne.

Slow-handclap game of football—the ball bigger than himself—Garbo awoke to the slap of the waves against the hull of his boat, the dance of light and the fiddle squeal of gulls.

For a moment, he huddled in his blankets before easing himself from his bunk. The cold knifed through the grey track suit he wore as pyjamas. He pulled on a heavy-knit blue sweater.

Time for a long-service leave in a warmer country.

The decision cheered him, resolving days of lethargy, aftermath to the sick exhilaration of the kill. Where away?

South.

The world was coming apart as usual according to the boisterous voice of Radio Clyde. But his world—and the weather—were set fair. No further mention of the gamekeeper and the stag. A nine-day wonder on radio, television and in the tabloid headline:

ROGUE STAG
GORES GAMIE

He finished off the last of the cornflakes. While he did, he reviewed his readiness: stocked up on provisions. He'd have to stow them.

First things first: he checked his cover passport—British, Jeffrey Courtney, developer—to make sure his photograph under the tricky strip of clear plastic was okay. He left it on the cabin table while he took the sniper rifle from the guitar. He unloaded it and undid the screws on the hinge he'd twisted hitting the McAdam. The hinge he hammered flat again before re-screwing it in place.

Two of the screws on the bolt had been loosened by the impact. He tightened them and before stripping and oiling the rifle.

The cleaning gear, he stowed back in its locker near the engine housing. The rifle he repacked inside the guitar, and hung the guitar in its case. The provisions he sorted onto the table ready for stowing.

'Ahoy, Ocean Drummer.'

Garbo didn't care for the voice: its mix of cheeriness and authority. When he got on deck, a clinker-built rowboat was snugged up to the stern of his boat. In it were a uniformed cop and two passengers.

Plainclothes detectives.

Garbo gestured them aboard and they introduced themselves: Detective Inspector Alec Kelvin, narrow eyes and a pickled nose under a brown snapbrim, Detective Constable Moira Rankin, black hair so tightly French-rolled it resembled a truncheon and Police Constable John Archie Allison, a big guy whose shoulders were stretching his tunic to splitting point.

He ran his hand over the stainless steel tubular hoop which Garbo had been added to the boat's traditional wooden spoked wheel. 'My, it's the fine vessel you have here, Mr. Courtney, isn't it?'

Garbo agreed. 'I was about to boil the billy. Cup of tea?'

'That's very kind of you to be sure.' Allison spoke with a lilt, his English inspired by the rhythms of a more musical language.

Kelvin relaxed from a reluctant sourness to let's-wrap this. 'No need to take up any more of your time than necessary.' He'd been given a shit chase. Envy. Just because he was transferring to the best: the London Metropolitan Police Force. 'Absolutely no need.' What he meant was that he didn't want to waste any more of his time because the plod who'd got him into the shit chase fancied a cup of tea. 'Understand you go fishing?'

Wouldn't it? Garbo thought. Run wild in a crowded street and everyone's blind. Quiet outing in a lonely place and someone sees you. He said: 'Nothing like a fresh fish fry-up.'

'Night of the fifteenth.'

'That was the night of the storm,' Garbo said. 'Got caught near Inverary.'

'A right wild night it was,' Allison said. 'Aye, and a right sad one.'

Kelvin gestured him into silence. 'You didn't hear anything?'

'Only the fish,' Garbo said. 'Shit, have you ever heard fish laughing?'

'Shots, I meant.'

'In that storm?'

'It's asking a bit much, I agree. But Constable Allison here got a call about someone shooting up a camp. Killing a dog and giving its master a taste of rifle butt.'

'Who'd want to camp out at this time of year?'

'That we don't know. Constable Allison didn't get the informant's name,' Kelvin said. 'Or the name of anyone else for that matter. We do know groups of nutters come out from the city to play Rob Roy and his merry men.'

'And women.' Allison said. 'The informant was a woman.'

Garbo remembered the supple slip of a woman with the feral red hair. She'd wanted him to take her with him. Maybe she was still pursuing him. 'Cuppa,' he said. 'You sure you won't have a cup of tea?'

'A pee.' Detective Constable Moira Rankin said.

Garbo waved to the companionway. 'For'ard,' he said. 'You can't miss it.' And thought: the smell.

Ducking low, he followed her, Kelvin and Allison behind him. 'You're cosy enough.' Allison was surveying the main cabin: the provisions on the table, the rock-'n-roll pictures and the guitar in its plexiglass case. He was bloodhound slow. And alert. 'Musician are you?'

'Developer.' Kelvin waved the passport, a detective demonstrating his trained observation compared to that of a plod.

'That's right,' Garbo said.

'British passport,' Kelvin said. 'I'd've taken you for an Aussie.'

'Born here. Brought up there.'

Kelvin nodded. Garbo noted how his eyes lingered on the passport's front cover. It wasn't the gilt coat of arms he was admiring. It was the number he was memorising. As he'd memorised the contents.

'So,' Allison said. 'It's not the musician you are then?'

Garbo explained the *Ocean Drummer's* history as he lit the stove in the galley. He did not put on the billy. He put on a frying pan and whacked four rashers of bacon into it.

Allison was examining the brass plate dedicated to Wild Bill Weatherby. Kelvin was eyeing the provisions on the table. 'Oats to, keep body and soul together,' he said. 'Beans to blow them apart.' He'd taken off his snapbrim to reveal narrow strips of hair pasted across his pate like laces in a football.

Another hard comedian. Garbo'd thought his father was the only one. But Scotland was full of them: men whose aim was to get off set-piece jokes, eyes unrelenting: Laugh, or I'll chin you. Kelvin had moved on from his joke. He was saying: 'You don't happen to have a rifle?'

Garbo kept his eyes from the guitar. 'Fishing's my thing.'

'Any trouble with gamekeepers?'

'Sea fishing,' Garbo said. 'I haven't got a river licence.' Kelvin's eyes were comedian intent. 'You heard about the gamekeeper?'

Radio Clyde was still sound-papering the day. Garbo nodded towards it. 'I was surprised. Does it happen often?'

'Not very. In fact, Constable Allison here thinks it was strange, and said so in his very full report.'

'Indeed it is strange. Now if it had happened during the rutting season, the spring, well, yes. But at this time of the year ...'

Garbo found he had to see to the bacon. He returned to the main cabin at the same time as Rankin. She did not say anything. She didn't need to. Had she found anything for'ard, Garbo knew he would've been answering more pointed questions.

Kelvin had relaxed, a superior confident of having exposed the stupidity of an inferior. He led his team back on deck. Allison seemed reluctant to leave. 'Man, I envy you. I hear tell you're thinking of a sail to Arran.'

Garbo'd mentioned the possibility in the local store when buying his provisions. 'Or Islay,' he said. 'Visit the distilleries. Or maybe go up to Ardishaig, Lockgilpead and through the Crinan Canal.' His eyes passed over the ribbon Allison wore on his blue tunic: General Service Medal. 'Then south. Mooring's, Burnham-on-Crouch, handy for London.'

The sea gulls were squealing round a blue and white fishing boat coming into the stone quay of Tarbert with its sandstone and white-washed buildings backed by a rise of green hill. Kelvin and Rankin were already in the rowboat. Allison halted in his passage to it. 'Your bacon,' he said, 'You don't want your bacon burning on you.'

Garbo didn't mind if the bacon burned to a crisp as long as it killed the smell Allison must surely know.

The sea gulls kept squealing, diving and rising in, an ecstasy of hunger.

And a bird more strange twittered: the mobile phone at Garbo's belt.

First call only. But he had to answer it. 'Give me a break. It may be your idea of a dream house. That doesn't mean it's mine, mate. I'll get back to you when—if—I can work out the finance.' He thumbed the mobile off. 'Real estate agents,' he said to them. But it was Allison he had to convince. 'Part vulture, part hyena and all fox, trying to sell me a house in London. Okay, I do need a bigger place. Will the bastard give me a chance to think about it? Calls morning, noon and night.'

– 27 –

Hurlingham Club, London, S.W.6

Rex D'Acre bent from the saddle on the wooden horse and swung his polo mallet in an arc. The mallet thwacked fairly on the ball which rattled against the wire mesh of the practice cage.

Three hundred up.

He hit two hundred more before dismounting. He knew his limitations as a rider but believed in the power of practice if not to make perfect, then at least to make competent.

He'd seen Kerry Packer play—a top-heavy centaur who scored when it counted. Next season he himself would play—here, and at Windsor Great Park—exchange chukka chat with H.R.H. Over his red polo shirt and his white jodhpurs, D'Acre put on a blue club blazer. For a moment, he sat in his Lancia gazing across the Thames to Wandsworth, the towers of its jail a world away from the green enclave of the club where a redolence of the raj lingered in Hurlingham House, its lake, polo field, running track, tennis courts and cricket ground, the ease of its members.

None greeted D'Acre. He had the loner's ability to isolate himself. He started the Lancia's engine to get its heater going as his sweat chilled. His analysis of the Prince's Trust, particularly its Conclusion, had, he felt sure found favour.

Indeed, it appeared to him that further analyses would not be unwelcome. This he had anticipated. From his blazer pocket, he took a draft of his Submissions on *Post-Marital Options.*

'Comment on the post-marital futures of His Royal Highness, the Prince of Wales, and his spouse Her Royal Highness, the Princess of Wales, has tended to focus on, the prospect of divorce with all its costs, psycho-sexual, socio-political and, not least, financial.

'This tendency has come to dominate both public debate and the thinking of those whose duty it is to influence the debate in the interest of monarchical continuities.

'It appears to have been forgotten that there is an historically valid alternative to divorce which offers more crucial protection of those continuities particularly as they relate to the "mystic reverence" identified by Walter Bagehot as intrinsic to the Monarch's role as head of the Church of England, remarriage in that church of divorced persons being, of course, forbidden.

'Annulment as opposed to divorce would not vitiate the Monarch's headship of the Church of England which, it may be worth remarking, came into existence after Pope Clement VII refused to grant Henry VIII an annulment of his marriage to Katharine of Aragon on the grounds that the papal dispensation under which he married her, she being his brother Arthur's widow, was itself invalid. Annulment not divorce, *pace* the ignorant, is in a sense the bezel on which the Church of England turns.

'Accordingly, annulment would surely be a more positive option for His Royal Highness, the Prince of Wales, and a more benign option for Her Royal Highness, the Princess of Wales. Nor would an annulment affect the status of H.R.H., Prince William or H.R.H. Prince Henry.'

D'Acre re-read his Submission. He was privy to allegations about nuisance calls from H.R.H. the Princess of Wales to an art dealer called Oliver Hoare and a closer relation between her and a galloping major of sorts, one James Hewitt, both it appeared successors to her telephone swain, James Gilbey, allegations already scented by the creep hounds of Fleet but which had not yet set them baying for the benefit of the public.

He'd noted H.R.H.'s tendency to underline words for emphasis and pondered whether he should do the same. He decided against. Imitation might be the sincerest form of flattery. In relation to royalty, it had to be deployed with care.

Fine for a royal to emphasise meanings for a lesser mortal but not necessarily politic for such a mortal to emphasise meanings for a royal.

Should he bolster his Submission by referring to the allegations. Again, he decided not to. It would be otiose to refer to material on which a view had already been formed. His aim was to influence at whatever cost final outcomes, thus maintaining monarchical continuities while covering himself against the possibility of recrimination while seeking preferment.

His route to St James's Palace took him along Kings Road, its shops garish yet desperate, its music raucous-'n'-dole. He was cocooned from them—and from gaudy passersby. The Lancia's stereo system filled his mind with the raptures of the mysteries of *The Magic Flute.*

On an impulse—no, a compulsion—he drove towards Knightsbridge, passing Harrods on the way. What a spectacular bazaar it had become under the eager Mohammed Al Fayed.

Everything from a coffin to a honeycomb.

He acknowledged the salute of the uniformed policeman on duty at the entrance to Kensington Palace Gardens: Embassy Row. He slowed as he passed Kensington Palace itself. The Princess Diana's home. He'd heard her quip—the world had—about being 'The Prisoner of Wales'.

How many had heard the counter quip? 'She's not exactly in solitary confinement.'

He turned to drive back, and a green Harrods delivery van

approaching the palace forecourt almost collided with him.

The van driver deserved a reprimand. D'Acre got out of the Lancia and was accosted. Not by the van driver who went on into the forecourt.

'Mr. D'Acre?' Odd little person. Nose like Pinnochio's sister. Houndstooth cape. Bloodhound. 'Margot Seymour, *Crown.*'

Bloodhound with a tape-recorder. 'You're visiting Di then?'

'If you mean Her Royal Highness, the Princess of Wales, not today.'

Someone else'd been a-visiting: Simon Delamere. Margot Seymour pounced. 'Simon, darling, I heard you were on calling terms. Do tell.'

Without even a, 'No comment', Delamere pushed past her. D'Acre opened the passenger seat door for him and drove off. 'How opportune,' he said. It was. Since his El Vino assessment of Delamere he'd been wondering how to arrange a re-meet.

'Took a cab,' Delamere said. 'Drop me off, if you would.'

D'Acre pulled up, reached into the glove box and gave Delamere a red and black cap. 'I did tell you that a new distinction was in train. Your visit confirms your right to it.'

'She liked something I wrote,' Delamere said. 'And thanks.' D'Acre waved dismissively. 'Think nothing of it.'

From the Lancia's stereo, Mozart's music rose to a crescendo. D'Acre thought of what might have been: joining the Princess Diana's staff.

Her latest thing, he'd heard, was to favour tactile people. Whatever he was, he was not that.

Ghastly Yankee notion.

Was Delamere a tactile person?

– 28 –

Ocean Drummer, Loch Fyne

Garbo and his boat slipped down-loch in a pre-dawn darkness so intense that he could see the phosphorescence of fish seeking to escape the menace of his hull.

No way had he ever really meant to go by the Crinan Canal. All he needed was to be caught in a lock of a centuries old waterway by a plod like John Archie Allison.

He made the Sound of Bute as dawn broke, loosing an easterly. The boat heeled, lifted and swooped as he got it under sail. To port was the Isle of Bute. Ahead to starboard was the Isle of Arran, its peak Goatfell, shadowy.

Dead ahead was the stern of a ship heading as he was into broad estuary of the Clyde.

Panama tramp.

That was his plan. Sail the seven seas and the five oceans. He sipped at the bowl of soup he'd made: Baxter's Spicy Thai Chicken with Lemon Grass. A taste of where he intended to sail. Might need a bit more money. No point in returning to Vietnam or Australia except in style. He'd checked his Z-for-Zurich numbered account. He was still short of the million he always wanted. Maybe he should collect what Pink 'Un, the Pom owed him. Then he'd be set for life.

And when he'd had enough of sailing or it became too much.

Boom!

The block of Composition 4 would see him off.

No trace left of his boat.

Nor of him.

What was it God-awful Gough'd said when he brought the last of the Viet vets home.

'Unhonoured.'

'Unsung.'

'Unwept.'

Same to you, Garbo thought. And may dingos piss on your tombstone.

He looked astern. No chance of catching a last glimpse of Greenock. Kern'd been surprised at its being nominated as RV. He should've told Kern about the ghosts: his father's story of the ghosts swimming, not in the shallow waters of the firth of Clyde, way out in the deep channel. How his father and his pals, down from Glasgow on a bike run, had watched the ghosts emerge from the channel and come bounding through the grey-white shallows to vanish into a clump of elderberry bushes.

To stand forth tall: ghosts from Gallipoli in their slouch hats who went away into the bright gloaming as if their courage had won them the right to the sunlight of the faraway land to which they were returning.

Years later facts had come together more powerfully than any ghosts: Greenock was the birthplace of William Bridges who raised the First Australian Imperial Force; the swimmers not Gallipoli ghosts, members of the Second Australian Imperial Force, temporarily in Scotland during World War Two.

So powerfully did the facts come together that his father'd volunteered for the Australian Army—its greatest battalion, Third Royal Australian Regiment, which held a main Chinese thrust south at Kapyong in Korea.

Forgotten battle.

Forgotten wounds.

His father forgot his. Invalided out, he became a dogman, riding girders into place on the end of a crane hawser.

Until his fall.

'Bastard!' he yelled into the freshening wind. 'Bastard!' And his yell echoed from storied hills among which is one known as The Sleeping Warrior.

The Panama tramp—MV *Viking Conquest*—was picking up speed. He was in no hurry. Long service leave. Pink 'Un, the Pom could go piss himself. Garbo brought the boat onto a new tack.

No way he was going to work for a balls-up artist who owed him.

– 29 –

Golden Square, London, W.1

Guy Jessop, stretched on his green leather couch, felt his scarred eye twitch.

Relax.

He took a series of deep breaths. He'd done the same in his fox-hole while an Argie patrol tried to home in on his signals.

It'd worked better there than here. If he took any more bloody breaths, he'd hyperventilate. He stood up and forbore to check the time. He'd checked it less than fifteen minutes before.

What a monumental cock-up. His name was all over it. He should not have broken his rule by contacting Garbo to take on a second successive task.

Dietrich a no-show.

A never again.

Caught by a couple of fellow pros, one spotting his obsessive fire on a sniper alley used by civilian rabbits, the other laying down mortar fire to stonker him.

Jessop glanced at his drinks table. No mixing liquor with the Bennies he'd taken. Maybe Valium would've been better.

Bolshie Garbo out of line, instead of ignoring the first mobile call, waiting for a second and then heading for the nearest public telephone box, he'd responded.

The charade about a house.

Ad lib cover obviously. For whose benefit? Casual visitors?

Garbo didn't have visitors, casual or otherwise. He had a detached, fit coldness that repelled without words, as it made him a natural whose training'd made him unstoppably sure.

What was it Australians said? 'Mad as a meataxe.'

All more or less mad: Australians. The distance? The belief that sunshine had transmuted them from old-lag Poms into golden leaders of Asia?

Mad.

Sad.

The El Caliph Room: Top of the Ambassador Hotel. Kowloonside. Celebration of the end of Operation Styx against a triad, exploiting the synergy of sex and drugs.

Garbo'd knocked the triad taipan. Nine hundred if an inch. Crosswind, heralding a typhoon.

Deep in the post-action piss-up: too little grub, too much booze, Jessop'd suggested the secret of Garbo's marksmanship must be zen. 'You know, zen masters can will their arrows to the target?'

'I know. But zen's not my secret.'

As the resident quintet, its three women in floral tea-gowns, its men in black tie sawed and hammered show tunes—*Oklahoma!*—with fiddles, xylophone, piano and double bass. Jessop gave to get: talking about his father, the Warrant Officer First Class. Garbo responded. 'First class, eh? Mine made corporal. Korea. Invalided out. Took a long fall. Survived. But brain damaged. Medico wanted me, next of kin, to countersign him into a loonybin.'

'You refused.'

'Should've strangled the benign bastard with his own stethoscope. Him and his bitch of an off-sider.'

Definitely mad as a meat-axe.

Absolute nutter.

On contract.

The telephone twittered. Jessop got the command bark into his voice. 'Where the hell've you been?'

'Here. And it is hell waiting for you.'

Emma.

'Sorry, darling. Thought you were the dastardly client I'm waiting to call me.'

'You've been there so long. At least forty-eight hours.'

'And the rest. Big contract.'

'I do wish you'd get some help in the office.'

'One volunteer is worth ten pressed men. Can I expect you tomorrow?'

'A full-time secretary's what I meant.'

Jessop had known what she meant. He preferred to make do with the endless supply of temps, one of the many boons of Thatcherism in Jessop's view, although he'd heard cynics suggest Maggie should be a temp: get a guardsman P.M. in. 'Later,' he said. 'Cash flow doesn't warrant it.'

'You always say that.'

'Must cut down on overheads. One of the cars, yours perhaps. Or school fees. Holland Park Comprehensive is still an option.'

'Do stop teasing. Leave a message on the answering thingummy asking your client to call here. I need you.'

'Impossible situation.'

It was. Jessop had to make contact with Garbo, his mobile off.

Still mad?

Or ...

'How long?' Emma was saying.

'As long as it takes,' he said. 'Then we'll celebrate.'

She didn't hear the second part. She'd hung up on the first.

He tried to sleep. Any nightmare would be better than his guess as to what had happened to Garbo.

Not casual visitors.

Police, who'd found a flaw in his previous gig.

If Garbo talked ...

Even Holland Park Comprehensive would not be an option. His sons might end up living in his Hornsey safe house and attending a ragged, papist school.

Not to mention the reason for Emma's eagerness to have him home. He sat up, swung his feet to the floor and bent over. She believed she was pregnant with a girl. She'd been right about the boys—said she could always tell after the ultimate orgasm: the seed hitting the egg.

A daughter.

Sons you could send bare-arsed into the world, cock in hand. A daughter?

– 30 –

Cairnban, Lochgilphead, Argyll

Ropes, alpenstock, carabineers, crampons, pitons, boots, anorak, heavy woollen stockings, knee-breeches, sleeping bag, Bergen rucksack: John Archie Allison was checking his climbing gear in the living room-kitchen of his cottage home. Or re-checking, it was already in perfect order.

Working with Moira Rankin again, he'd been reminded of the mountain rescue course they'd done together in the Cairngorms with Glenmore Lodge as their base, she roped to him as their team traversed a snow and ice pitch.

Routine.

Ach, he was getting soft. He put the gear back in its storage chest near the front door, ready for the next time.

The television sat wall-eyed in the living room-kitchen. Not that he fancied it, depressed enough already from gazing into the fire, imagining he could see Moira Rankin with her bright hair down.

Moira Rankin.

Moira.

The penny dropped when he began polishing a pair of brass candlesticks. 'Dhia,' he said as if the Gaelic for God might redeem him from his own idiocy.

The penny was the smell of rifle oil associated forever in his memory with the smell of Brasso on tunic buttons and webbing buckles.

He finished polishing the candlesticks, a rare double-twist pair that had been given to his mother by his father and were therefore more precious than gold. He put new red candles in them before replacing them on the mantelpiece in the front room on either side of the mirror-framed wedding photograph of his parents, his father in his Black Watch uniform, his mother in white.

From the nearby Crinan Canal came the hoot of a boat going through. Maybe he might just have helped the penny to drop. He'd kept a look out for the *Ocean Drummer* and asked his neighbours about it. He was sure it had not gone through the canal. To double check, he made a telephone call to Tarbert.

Only then did he call Detective Inspector Alec Kelvin in Lochgilphead. 'You remember yon Mr. Courtney.'

'Yon who?' Kelvin said. 'I don't know about you, thing is I'm awful busy.'

'The one with the swank boat.'

'The point. The point. Get to the point.'

'You asked him did he have a rifle and he said no.'

'Not only did he say it, there wasn't a solitary sign of a rifle on the boat.'

'Aye, maybe. But there was the smell of one.

'Smell?'

'Rifle oil.'

Kelvin's eyes rolled; for a moment he looked like a dead-eyed statue. Tchoochter! He was a Lowlander with the Lowlander's contempt for the Highlander. 'You're telling me you could smell rifle oil on that boat.'

'The very same.' Allison couldn't resist a sly dig. 'Once you've smelt it, you can never forget it.'

'Bullshit,' Kelvin said. 'What about bullshit? Can anyone forget the smell of bullshit?'

Allison chuckled. Less at what Kelvin'd said than at what he himself was about to say. 'If you're all that busy, I can handle it myself.'

'Do that.'

'There's only one thing. You paid more attention to yon Mr. Courtney's passport than I did. If you would just let me be having his address and the passport number.'

Kelvin had a pro's reluctance to hand over information. 'Ask him yourself, why don't you?'

'He left his mooring at Tarbert yesterday.'

'I seem to remember him saying he was thinking of a sail to Arran, then south.'

'Early. Against the tide.'

'Okay. No need to spell it out in block capitals. I'll run a check on the passport.'

'You will be letting me know how it goes?'

'If you hear from me, it's a goer. If you don't.' Kelvin hung up. He *was* very busy, clearing his desk preparatory to his departure for the Met. Big crime, he believed, followed the big money. Big money, London. Big crime there. And big career opportunities.

He'd've computer checked the Courtney passport if the wee *deoch an doruis*—the farewell drink at the door—weren't as gigantic here. Unlike the computer facilities.

Not to worry. He was an adept, halfway to the Met. He accessed its MetComCop: Passport File.

Bingo!

The Courtney passport was one of a random-number list of five blanks missing from the main passport office, Petty France, London. He tried for the double bingo by keying in Jeffrey Courtney, developer. NK—nothing known.

Kelvin logged off. Time for the greater computer: the human

brain to take over. Rifle oil. What a hoot. Jeffrey Courtney reeked of something stronger than rifle oil.

Definitely an Aussie. No mistaking them. They wore chips on their shoulders the way South American generals wore epaulettes.

The fact that the passport was originally a blank surely meant that false identity wasn't a factor. Jeffrey Courtney, developer, needed a British passport to operate in Britain. Maybe Europe.

Some scam or other. Kelvin knew about scams. Kelvin knew about Aussies

Now he was more than halfway to the Met. He was heading for C6—Company Fraud Branch—at the Big House, New Scotland Yard. He crammed the last of his desk stuff into his briefcase and picked up an already packed suitcase.

Quiet holiday first.

Touch of the sun.

Drop of ouzo.

Final farewell.

He took the A83 north along the banks of Loch Fyne, aiming to turn the head of the loch at Cairndow and then head south for Glasgow Airport by way of the Clyde Tunnel.

Grand day for a drive. But that wasn't the half of it: maintaining a discreet tailing distance behind his black Peugeot 208 was Moira Rankin in her blue Golf.

She'd insisted on separate cars, not wanting to compromise her career.

Kelvin, the hard comedian, winked at himself in his rear-view mirror.

Her career.

That was the last thing on his mind.

– 31 –

Brodick, Isle of Arran

Like all predators, Garbo tended to relax when not in action. He was down to a tourist saunter and his earlier anger down to a quiet implacability when he found a red public telephone box, its interior warmed by the sun which had broken through the clouds and left the island's highest peak, Goatfell, wreathed in mist.

'Bay dahn aw pun yau,' he said when Jessop answered the phone. One of two Cantonese phrases he and Jessop used as sign and countersign when they were working together in Hong Kong. Bring the cheque to my friend. Jessop responded with the other phrase. *'Fo-kay, my dahn.'* Bring the cheque to me.

He then got the command bark going. 'Contact A.S.A.P's the rule, you know that.'

'You're dead-set lucky to hear from me at all, you mug. It's only you owe me.'

'Don't worry, I'll pay what I owe and more.'

'*Gay doa cheen,*' Garbo said. How much?

'Always ready to negotiate with a headliner.'

'I'm on long service leave.'

'How very colonial. More to the point, are you clear?'

'I'm always clear.'

'You've had fans to see you.'

'Two plain, one blue.'

'Thought as much when you started chattering about real estate, and then went off air. Fans of your previous gig?'

'Not fans. Just a general sniff around. No worries, my beard passed muster.'

'In that case, I've got a headliner spot. Long gig. Trio accompaniment.'

'Trio, eh? As it happens, I've been thinking of retirement, give the younger talent a chance.' Jessop tried for a laugh. 'You, and Dame Edna.'

'*Bloody ying gock yun!*'—Bloody Englishman.

'Give me a break. Not my order, your ad lib. Can't charge it, so fifty K. Plus seventy five k for the trio. That's entering. Ditto exiting. Plus ten k advance expenses. Buy yourself a nice retirement annuity.'

'Prefer superannuation.'

'Not after you check annuities, you won't.'

Garbo believed in fate.

And money.

'Two sixty total,' he said. 'Make it two eighty and I provide the props.'

'That's twenty for props. What're you proposing to use—a battle tank? Five's all I can manage.'

'Make it ten.'

'Done. Total, two-twenty.'

'You should'v been in the Pay Corps.'

'Was, as cover.'

'Fiddled your way out, as I think you've fiddled me.'

'Nice to have a comedian on the bill, especially in Ireland.'

'Now he tells me.'

'Re-contact on arrival for time, theatre and trio's costumes. And watch out for Hush Puppy fans.'

‘You should be on the bill with me.’

‘Yeah, it’s a great gig. You can’t miss.’

‘I never do.’

Jessop didn’t mind giving a second banana the final punchline as long as he had the margin. And it was a nice one. Almost as good as something in the city.

Garbo sauntered on up to the red sandstone pile of Brodick Castle. In its gardens the last of the rhododendrons flickered. From up there, he could make out Ireland. Could swim in, he thought. If the water wasn’t so bloody cold.

Making his way back down to the island’s ferry terminal off which he’d moored his boat, he began to work out more realistic possibilities for his infiltration phase.

And his ex-filtration.

– 32 –

Crown Liquor Saloon, Belfast

Michael MacLirr watched Pamela Fitzgibbon enter from Great Victoria Street, letting in a quick, wet bluster of the day and the unmistakable growl of an armoured personnel carrier amid the more peaceable traffic on the adjacent motorway. Like a swan, he thought. Unruffled by the weather. She wore a brown wig and a speckled tweed blouson top, green silk shirt and swirl of tweed skirt above knee-high brown boots.

From the long mahogany bar, its sheen matching his leather jacket, he went forward to greet her and to break the concentration of her survey of their meeting place. No kiss, though it would've been apt. He ushered her into the low partitioned snug he'd reserved, aware of the drop of the bar's decibel level and of the looks of every man and his grandfather there.

Envy mostly, except for the two in the blue donkey-jackets at the far end of the bar, one tall, long-haired and pink-cheeked, the other a grizzled, altogether bigger and harder nut.

Those pink cheeks. MacLirr smiled. Disguise himself as he might a certain kind of Englishman could not hide the bonny pink cheeks that bespoke generations of four, square meals, not recent tighteners—although MacLirr's Da always maintained the pinkness was down to Irish wet nursing.

'Share the joke,' Pamela Fitzgibbon was saying.

It was not a joke he could share with anyone, and leastways then and there with her. 'I was only thinking that Belfast has the best bar of all the world in this one,' he said. 'With the worst parliament up the road there in Stormont. The very worst. Had to be, otherwise why would the gang in Westminster have closed it down? Like the Mafia closing down the Camorra.'

She unbuttoned her blouson. Her silk shirt enhanced the green of her eyes but never the hint of a smile in them as he went on: 'Sure, the phony old Basil, Lord Brookeborough, set an imperial standard for Poobahs. What was it? One day a week, or two, at the office? Awarded the Military Cross for gallantry in the face of the enemy and his viscountcy for effrontery in the face of liberty.'

'Talking of offices, why the switch from your safe house to here?'

He'd expected that question. 'Because a safe house remains a safe house only as long as you don't make an unbreakable habit of meeting there. I've been thinking ...' He smiled. 'I've been thinking, our first meeting, the memory of it needs expunging.' He smiled again. Magnetic personality, she thought. And: has it never occurred to him that magnets can repel as well as attract?

'What about a bite to eat?' he said. 'The oysters here are fine, bred to drown happily in Guinness. Or there's ham if you fancy that. And potato salad.'

'Maybe I've had enough ham for the time being.' He guffawed at her taunt. She went on: 'Oysters, however, yes. With a Guinness. Potato salad, too.'

He stood up to call over the snug's partition for the food, adding ham for himself. His eyes went to the two donkey jackets at the end of the bar. The grizzled one was big enough to be a Fijian S.A.S. trooper who'd popped a few pills to make him look white enough to go under cover.

Seated again, MacLirr said: 'The latest from London is they're ready to talk with us—talk seriously. Or substantively, as they put it.'

'They don't put it that way. "Substantively" is White House-speak. The U.S. Government is playing to Irish-American Democrats.'

'The Brits, it's them who're talking to us, and isn't that the rare contradiction after their endless chatter about us being terrorists—unspeakable, untouchable, irredeemable?'

'The English will always talk to terrorists eventually. Irgun, Palestine, Mau Mau, Kenya, Eoka, Cyprus. They understand terrorism. What's their class system but polite terrorism? They send their children to boarding school to be terrorised.'

'Sure, you'd know about that now, wouldn't you?' She ignored the riposte. MacLirr held the door of the snug open for a waiter to serve their food. When he had gone, she said: 'Your minder's not here?'

He'd expected that question, too. 'He's having a bit extra training like you've had yourself.' MacLirr made a pistolling motion with the thumb and forefinger of his left hand. 'Now answer me this: the Brits, why so long?'

'Apart from the thunder and lightning of the good Dr. Ian Paisley and his ilk and the firepower of our loyalist opposite numbers, there's love-hate. Or admiration-hate. Or even self-hate admiration.'

'Love-hate, you say. Admiration-hate. Self-hate admiration. Which is it?' She was eating and drinking with the gusto he'd seen in women at harvest time. 'Which is it?' he said again. 'Why?'

'They don't know themselves. As to why, I think the English, and in a different way the Scots, know subconsciously that we held to the truth in the divide of the Reformation at considerable cost and they sold it out for considerable profit.'

'You mean?' He raised his Guinness and quoted the folk verse: 'Don't talk of your Protestant Minister/Or his Church without meaning or faith/For the foundation stone of his temple/Was the bollocks of

Henry the Eighth.'

'Neat if simplistic. The economic rewards of taking over church property were enormously significant, as significant as the enclosure of common land or the Highland Clearances.' She finished the brown bread that had been served with her oysters and started on her potato salad. 'Or even privatisation today. What's that if not the enclosure of common land by other means? Water's a community resource. So is electricity. And communications—Victorian capitalists knew that, otherwise they wouldn't have established the Post Office as a community resource.'

He was tempted to try to get another rise out of her by holding up his hand and saying, 'Please, sister, may I leave the room'. And would have except he needed to win her confidence. 'The Scots, you said, different.'

'Were and are. Their reformation didn't turn on the bollocks of Henry the Eighth or bags of loot to reduce his debts. They were more into the crucial theological question of predestination. Are we predestined to damnation or salvation?'

MacLirr realised the question was not rhetorical, and took refuge in a swallow of Guinness and a joke. 'Damned if I know.'

She did not smile. 'Predestined or not, the Scots did lose their independence to England after the Reformation. *Post hoc* or *propter hoc.* I'd say *propter hoc.* The faith of any nation is the essence of its nationality. The Scots changed their faith more substantially than the English and lost their independence equivalently. Irony. Irony. The Ulster Scots hold on to Nanny England now as their forebearss once held out against it. Instinct swings them back. The good Dr. Ian's their pope, infallible in politics if not in faith.'

He laughed. 'Isn't the same fella the grandest anti-pope of them all?'

'My point: anti-popes do tend to rant against true popes.' She gazed at his uneaten brown bread. 'Can I have that?'

He tore the bread in two and gave her half. 'You're obviously the religion expert.'

With the blunt side of her table knife, she rapped him across the knuckles. 'Any more of your teasing, and you're for the sharp edge.'

'Brief me, then about the Republic of Ireland Constitution and the status it guarantees to the Catholic Church. A stumbling block wouldn't you say?'

'No more than the special status granted to the Boaz Boys—Freemasons and all their works under the Northern Ireland Constitution—unless, of course, pseudo-religion has greater status than orthodox religion.'

'The pseudo may need political props more.'

'True. And the extent to which a political system supports the pseudo is the extent of its eventual implosion into a moral vacuum. Look at the Soviet Union as it was, with its pseudo-religion Marxism and Saints Lenin and Stalin.'

Vaccinated with a gramophone needle, he thought. Or maybe overdoing her cover, gabbing on. And said: 'Sum up, if you would. Does London mean it this time whether in love-hate or whatever?'

'Hope beats love-hate. There again, the Orange card has trumped hope before.' She finished the bread and the last of the Guinness. 'You know my question.'

He did. She'd asked it at each of their meetings. He shook his head: no sign of anyone who might be the ruffian hired to chastise journalists.

Or worse.

The two donkey-jackets were still at the end of the bar when he left the snug with her: Hush Puppies, plain clothes members of the Redhill

Sports and Social Club. He'd shown them the merchandise. Now he had to find a way of getting the merchandise to a place where it could be safely lifted in accordance with the bargain.

At the exit they separated, and he watched her sway into the wind and rain, waving for a taxi. Somehow he had to win her complete confidence. He'd caught her looking at him—those green eyes—as if she'd turned over a stone to find the last snake in all Ireland.

– 33 –

World's End, London, S.W.10

Rex D'Acre's very private residence was one he'd retained after investing in a spread of properties in the 1970s and selling them profitably in the 1980s when Prime Minister Margaret Thatcher, true to her surname, waved her fiscal hand to put a mortgaged roof over so many heads.

In real-estate speak, 'renovator's delight' described the exterior, 'bijou' its interior, the former providing a measure of security for the latter. D'Acre was especially fond of the white-panelled study where he kept his collection of rare books, among them copies of Henry St John, Lord Bolingbroke's, *The Idea of a Patriot King,* the 1744 edition, bound in calf, which Alexander Pope had secretly printed, and the 1749 edition corrected by the author. D'Acre preferred this. Not only was it bound in fine shagreen, it bore the Bolingbroke crest.

He took it from the ebony bookcase. Here was a treatise written in the eighteenth century which still had relevance for the twentieth century. And the twenty-first. Europe, innately monarchical, would need a unifying symbol then as it needed one in the eighth and ninth centuries when Charlemagne emerged.

How could H.R.H. Prince Charles, in whose veins flowed the blood of that great, that legendary Charles, fail to be influenced by a work which had so strongly inspired George III, the ancestor he was at such pains to defend against the diagnosis of madness?

D'Acre checked a remembered precept addressed to the Patriot

King against the text in his hand. ‘Espouse no party ... govern like the common father of his people.’

Too soon, D’Acre thought, too soon perhaps to be making a further Submission. He poured himself a Hine cognac and carried it and the book into his bedroom. When he next made a Submission, he would be suggesting an elaboration of the precept: eschew espousal of any particular party and also any particular faith.

On the wall facing his bed was a gilt-framed portrait of H.R.H., the Princess Diana, which he had painted himself from a favourite photograph. White, her colour: Royal Aphrodite in sea-foam white, her swimmer’s shoulders rising from it. Her neck, her ears adorned with pearls. How casually she offset her priceless tiara by leaning forward, clasping her knees and smiling like a schoolgirl caught dressing up in her mother’s ball gown.

He checked another remembered quotation against the text and gazed at the portrait. It was surely the destiny of H.R.H. the Princess Diana to make her husband, ‘the most popular man in his country and a patriot king at the head of a united people’.

Below the portrait was a black marble pedestal on which was a white candle in a silver holder. Rex D’Acre lit the candle, switched off the bedroom lights and raised his glass of cognac to the portrait.

Exquisite.

The pleasure of secret knowledge.

The Jessop contact number. The metallic voice saying cryptically: ‘The show is on.’

Soon he would have another photograph, a prime print, to form an iconic diptych. He threw his empty cognac glass into the bedroom fireplace where it shattered. He’d remembered the Harrods van at Kensington Palace. And a later hint: the eager Mohamed Al Fayed, friend of the Princess Diana’s father, had a son, Dodi.

Film producer.

Playboy.

And no doubt a tactile person.

Would he recall the Treason Act of 1351, promulgated to protect the integrity of the Plantagenet line and since used to protect its successor lines—Tudor, Stuart, Hanover, Saxe-Coburg-Gotha and Windsor—embodied in their chief members including the wife of the Monarch's son and heir.

High treason.

A capital offence punished by a masked executioner.

And masked executioners were still part of the apparatus of sovereignty.

Honourable Free Masons would deem his gross abuse of the Craft off the square, and castigate him as they'd castigated Propaganda Due—P2—for its Vatican activities, based on the premise: what is the point of a secret society if it cannot use its secrecy secretly?

His ruffian in waiting was behind the arras.

With his right hand, D'Acre lifted a long shard of the glass from the fireplace. He slashed the shard across his left hand, drawing blood and smeared the blood across the portrait.

Time to abort?

– 34 –

Checkpoint, Zulu Fermanagh

Garbo should've known better. He'd been party to a similar, random tactic himself. His crossing of the border from the Republic of Ireland into Northern Ireland in his hired Rover Quintet had been a formality, confirming his confidence in his cover and his belief that he'd conducted a model infiltration.

Now on the reverse slope of the hill he'd driven up was breathtaking view of Upper Lough Erne.

And an armoured personnel carrier angled across the road to make it single-lane: A.P.C. and a mix of Royal Ulster Constabulary and British infantry. His first impulse was to reverse and get out of there.

Behind the stone wall in the key ground to his left, a flanking soldier had him in the telescopic sights of his weapon. Garbo had also done this on occasions: most effective way of taking a close look, and if you didn't like what you saw.

Bang!

Model infiltration, my arse. Garbo let the irony cool him. He'd tried. His initial plan: short course from the north, Larne, Belfast itself, or by Lough Foyle to Derry. No go. He would come under intense perimeter security. Sailing further by way of Lough Swilly to Letterkenny, Donegal would put him in the republic but with almost as much risk from covert trans-border surveillance.

South beyond Dublin, he'd sailed, and found safe mooring within the stone curve of Arklow's breakwater harbour. Unvandalised public phone for Pink 'Un re-contact to get the gen on theatre and trio costumes.

Kit, smart-casual, hair, sea-tousled, he'd made himself known to Customs and Gardai; he'd visited the local tourist spots: Glendalough and Powerscourt. Provisions he'd bought in the local store and drinks in the local pub, telling the smiling customers, among them the Gardai Sergeant, Seumus McNulty, that he was off to explore Dublin and ancestral links, only the amount of his cover story needed at this stage.

On the N3 out of Dublin he'd picked up extra cover, waiting amid pastures as green as a drought-ridden, bank-ridden Aussie grazier's dream of heaven.

Only thing green about the checkpoint infantrymen was in the mottling of their combat camouflage. Its dried-blood brown accorded more with their handling of their SA80 automatic rifles.

Guerrilla-war hardened as Garbo himself was: jungle not urban. Explained why the Pommy reluctantance to let go here. They had the world's toughest live-ammo urban warfare school: warfare of the future. Serbians, he'd heard, trained on pigs.

And Poms trained on Paddies. The cops—dark, bulky anoraks, Kevlar flak jackets, Sterling SMGs—impressed him more. They had the bleak eyes of men who hadn't seen a friend in years and if they did see one, he might put a bullet in them.

Garbo laid his passport on the front passenger seat ready for inspection. Behind him, his extra cover giggled: backpackers Gudrun Martz and Marga Hetzer, blonde, twin-like in denim and giant hiking boots. They were consulting a map to see how far it still was to their ultimate destination: Belfast, where they planned a peaceful, quiet time with the family of a demobbed Irish soldier, Gudrun had met in Berlin.

Twisting round in his seat, Garbo said: 'Better get your papers ready.' His eyes went to his guitar lying in its display case along the rear-window ledge. 'The cops'll love the fact you're going to Belfast for peace and quiet.'

'It cannot be any worse than Beirut,' Gudrun said.

Each took a passport from the leather pouch she had hung round her neck as Garbo drove forward a vehicle length. The vehicle ahead of him—Jeep Cherokee—had a stars and stripes sticker on its rear.

Suddenly, its door was being wrenched open and its driver—red ski-jacket, Levis and black jump boots—was straddled against the vehicle getting all-over measurement treatment, including inside leg. 'Yes, sir,' a Kevlar cop was saying. 'You can have my name and number. Hear me though: no fascist pig cheek. Not even under your breath.'

The straddled driver was trying to conjure with the name Kennedy. 'If you mean Jack, shag him as he shagged so many,' Kevlar man was saying. 'If you mean Jackie, how come a woman like that-married a shit like him when she could've had me for the asking.'

'The Senator,' the driver was saying. 'Senator Ted Kennedy.'

'Him? If I'd arrested him, he'd still be inside. And I don't mean a fancy-woman.'

'Outrage.'

'Rage away, laddie,' the Kevlar cop said, shepherding the Yank back into his Cherokee. 'None of your Teddy's driving now.'

Mug, Garbo thought. He'd roused the cops and the infantrymen; a routine check had become adrenalin charged. Their fingers were still off the triggers. Their attitudes said clearly: who's next for scalping?

Garbo.

Gudrun and Marga kept giggling as he drove the Rover slowly into the inspection zone, glancing at the white-on-red notice leaning against the APC.

SECURITY FORCES REGRET
ANY INCONVENIENCE OR DELAY
BLAME THE TERRORISTS

The Kevlar cop who took Garbo's passport wasn't missing anything even though Gudrun and Marga were proffering their passports, giggles and the rest.

He went through the drill: eyed flicking from the passport photograph to Garbo's face.

Would he recognise in it the been-there hardness that was in his own?

'We stretch our legs,' Gudrun said. She and Marga got out of the Rover. Tough cookies from sunnier climes, legs brown.

Kevlar cop was still intent on Garbo's passport. And one of the infantrymen spotted the guitar. 'Fender?'

'One-off special,' Garbo said. 'Belonged to Wild Bill Weatherby.'

'The session man? What a musician. Played right-hand guitar left-handed—like Jimi Hendrix.'

'That's him.' Garbo had rehearsed this scenario. What he hadn't rehearsed was the infantryman's next remark : 'How much?'

'Ten.'

'I'll have it.' The infantryman was caught between his weapons discipline and his wallet.

'Ten thou,' Garbo said. 'Wild Bill trashed guitars worse than Jimi Hendrix, and you probably know how bad he was.'

'Worst and best.'

Kevlar cop, looked on with grim indulgence: they came these British soldiers, they saw without conquering their daftness. 'You'll be wanting to give us a tune,' he said.

'Feel free,' Garbo said. 'Amp box would help.'

The infantryman opened the rear door of the Rover, aiming at least to touch the guitar.

Giggles. Squeals. Guffaws.

Into the air floated a pink balloon. And a black balloon. Then another brighter balloon, released by Marga. This one farted off briefly and fell limply on the road: a yellow condom.

Behind a vehicle hooted once. A second vehicle repeated the hoot. And a succession of vehicles joined in.

Kevlar cop, waved Garbo forward with his Sterling. And the infantryman slammed the rear door shut, his eyes on the guitar.

Gudrun and Marga caught up with the Rover beyond the inspection zone. 'We did that in Beirut,' Gudrun said.

Rain fell, softening the outlines of a strongpoint so that its steel stockade and meshed-topped concrete watchtower took on a semblance of a wood and daub fort of long ago.

– 35 –

Aldergrove Airport, Belfast

Jack Birton came in on the earliest flight ex-London, remembering the ancient joke about putting watches back three centuries. Or was it eleven centuries, and sundials, not watches?

In his own case, fifteen years was nearer the mark. Not that much seemed to have changed. The weather was still set stormy and the loom of Black Mountain as menacing as ever.

He was cheered when he dumped his gear at the Murray's car-hire desk and the woman gave him the full, 'Mr Birton, Rapix Worldwide' treatment. That was down to Connie. She had a way on the telephone of implying that Rapix Worldwide had recently swallowed Reuters and was moving in on News Limited before taking over Time-Warner. He began to fill out the car-hire forms.

'Cock-a-doodle-do!'. Birton completed the forms and took the car keys before turning to confront Simon Delamere who said: 'Climbing the ladder of success as a photo-journalist, I hear.'

Birton flicked at the Olympus camera, Delamere wore over his sheepskin jacket. 'I know they say it's foolproof. Is it you proof?

'Saw you on the plane.' Delamere grinned. His exes obviously did not cover the repair of his picket-fence teeth. 'You were reading. Incredible the way you synchronise your lips and your finger. What happens when you write.'

'Piss off.'

Birton knew he'd lost the rally by resorting to crudity. So did Delamere, and expected a prize. 'What about giving me a lift to the Europa?' He meant the city's main hotel, caravanserai for the hundreds of media types who came and went covering the war that was formally undeclared and yet as vicious as rape.

'Can't.' Birton swung his black camera-bag, labeled, X-RAY SENSITIVE, onto his shoulder, conscious as always of his Pentax and Nikon cameras. He picked up his suit bag. 'I've got other things to do.'

'Buy a pencil with a rubber on the end?' Delamere said. A low blow. Birton was picking up his Apple laptop in its black padded bag, also labelled, X-RAY SENSITIVE. Delamere moved off. 'I'll get a cab.'

'Don't forget to credit the cabbie in your story,' Birton said. 'Another one of your "Whither Ulster" pieces.'

'Oh, I think we can do better than that, the political entity with which we're dealing is Northern Island not Ulster.' Delamere waved his hand, two fingers, three, four, the lot. 'See you in the Europa bar. You owe me a drink after failing to buy at El Vino.'

Typical Delamere, leaving that point to last. Git. He made sure Delamere was headed towards the taxi rank to pick up one of the black shuttle cabs which were as special to Belfast as yellow cabs to New York, tuk-tuks to Bangkok or Jeepneys to Manila.

As Birton made his way to his hire-car—a beige Volvo—he tried to recast the outcome of the encounter; Delamere had assumed they would be seeing each other again in the Europa. Birton unlocked the Volvo. At least he hadn't been wearing his special red and black cap. Delamere would have been onto the significance of its red crown quicker than a flea on a poodle.

He kept his eye on the rearview mirror. Amazing Delamere's instincts and he was quite capable of saying: 'Follow that Volvo.

No black cab showed in the mirror. Ahead was the checkpoint,

Birton remembered from fifteen years before. He rummaged in one of the pockets of his black anorak. He pulled on the special red and black cap. The Royal Ulster cops could've been the guys of fifteen years ago: as implacable as the Black Mountain.

But the squaddies ... Birton got his eye on one. For a moment he thought the British Army must've decided to put women into the sharp end. Then he realised that under the camouflage helmet and battle-gear was a boy, a fresh-faced boy who could've been the son—grandson—of one of the squaddieq he'd first seen here. The senior cop glanced at Birton's papers, including his Buckingham Palace accreditation. His eyes fastened on the red crown. He stepped back. And saluted.

'Mind if I knock off some pix?' Birton said. The cop nodded. Birton took a Nikon shot of him. Plus shots of his colleagues and the squaddies, including the fresh-faced boy.

Leaving the checkpoint, Birton was thinking: 'A Terrible Beauty.' Connie was right. She'd mentioned Yeats, quoted the line, 'A terrible beauty is born', and suggested a picture-spread with the line as its theme might be a goer.

Clever girl.

She'd also emphasised that the Rapix travel budget was going bust on one-story trips. 'We've got to get at least two stories on each ticket.'

He'd been thinking the same thing himself for years. Now he was doing it. Was that the secret of woman power: the obvious? He grinned to himself. Well, that and the other obvious.

– 36 –

Queen's University, Belfast

From experience, Michael MacLirr knew that a rendezvous in a swimming pool was the best way to circumvent one kind of bugger. As he surfaced from an underwater lap of the university pool into the babble and splashing echoing from its tiled walls, he was certain that no electronic surveillance gear would be able to pick up anything he said.

In one clean heave, he lifted himself from the chlorine-green waters of the pool which steamed in the colder air. And no one could come wired up in bathing trunks. He tugged at his own green trunks as he moved to the hot shower arrea where Simon Delamere was waiting: well-lunched paunch big enough to hide a recording gismo. Fat chance. MacLirr grinned. He and Delamere went back to before paunches: students at the university when the Troubles regenerated in the late 1960s, initially as a civil rights movement—Delamere an eloquent leader, MacLirr an enthusiastic follower. The Royal Ulster Constabulary baton charges politicised them on different sides of the fault line. Or bloodline. Still they'd kept in touch across a bridge of bitter jokes, on MacLirr's side involving references to blue noses tending to become brown, and on Delamere's, jests about taigs book-worming their way to the bottom of the heap.

Less bitterness now. Mutual advantage. MacLirr led off with the thoughts of Pamela Fitzgibbon as if they were his own. Delamere, taken with the notion that 'substantive' indicated Washington input into London thinking said: 'Irish-Americans still care about outcomes here. And American politicians—particularly Democrats—sympathise, unlike Australian politicians. I'm just back from Down Under. By and large, even Irish-Australian Labor politicians don't appear to give a stuff. Too busy playing kiss-arse. If it's not Kerry Packer, it's Rupert Murdoch. They were even getting round to Conrad Black but he didn't understand local kiss-arse protocol and farted in their faces.'

'There's another matter,' MacLirr said. 'Royalty.'

'You mean to what extent should it be factored into the future?'

'Something like that.'

'It's of no consequence. Or very little.'

'No? Very little? So why are you and your rivals ready to pay such enormous sums for royal stories? You're not telling me the sums are inflated.'

'The money's real enough—or as real as any money is these days.'

'Still the dismal, economics philosopher. I thought you were into class punditry—chattering class—not petty-cash keeping.'

'I can match anyone else's price—and have done—for the right story.'

'No more of that', MacLirr said. 'Or it's split-sides surgery I'll be needing. Last time we ate, it was McDonald's although I'll bet that wasn't the name that went on your swindle sheet.'

Delamere stepped from under his shower. 'Only way to test a market: if you've got something, offer it for sale.'

MacLirr waited a moment before following Delamere towards the dressing rooms.

He did have something for sale.

Could he sell it to Simon Delamere? He felt sick that it was not virtue which preventing him answering his own question. It was foreknowledge: Delamere would be able to reciprocate the contempt heaped on him for betraying his youthful idealism.

MacLirr and Delamere left the mellow brick enclave of their university separately as they'd arrived, but now bound in a new complicity. 'You've got my contact numbers,' Delamere said. 'Any time, any reason.'

– 37 –

Quirk's Hotel, Enniskillen

Garbo had dropped the denim twins, Gudrun and Marga, in Beleek at the head of Lower Lough Erne where they wanted to buy pottery for their prospective hosts in Belfast.

He was thinking, he told them, of visiting Bundoran across the border. Instead he'd doubled back by quiet roads and green fields through Garrison, Manorhamilton and Belcoo to his theatre of operation.

An impressive memorial of United Kingdom wars: infantry man, head bowed over reversed rifle. Not Vietnam, Korea. The name always a button for hatred of the benign bastard who'd loonybinned his father.

The Korea hero.

Garbo relished the hatred. He needed it as much as adrenalin or ammo.

His reconn made it clear that the dress-circle buildings, including the St Michael's Reading Rooms, near the war memorial were too vulnerable for sniping positions. All were within pistol return-fire range and would also be within any immediate security cordon.

Bandit country and, as he'd learned in Vietnam, if pleasant landscapes made you blur reality, there was always the chopper clatter to remind you of security.

Or here, an encounter with a black Jaguar: driver, one passenger in the rear. 'Are we right for the Police Training Centre?' Plainclothes cop, the driver. Even making a polite inquiry, he had jail-key eyes. 'Straight ahead,' Garbo said. 'Left at the crossroads. You can't miss it.'

He wondered as he got into his Rover, and drove off what might have happened had he not briefed himself on the area. Would the cop've asked more pointed questions? Questions, like the first, inspired by instinct?

Garbo's own instinct was to harbour up. He'd spotted a GUEST PARKING sign, and a lane off a street which an ivied hotel fronted. At the lane's end a cobbled yard and what had been a coach-house set at right angles to the rear of the hotel. Further on, the lane intersected a main road: the A4, leading to the M1 and Belfast.

On top of the coach-house, a dovecote, its denizens fluttering and cooing home to roost. The coach-house doors hung askew, six-vehicle space, two occupied: mint-condition Morgan sports car with polished bonnet strap nest to a dilapidated Irish jaunting car. Garbo parked the Rover alongside them.

The hotel manager, Robert Walton, had grog-poached eyes. Garbo took in the suede-patched, fawn Pringle's cardigan, blue shirt, polka-dot cravat and cavalry-twill strides and Walton's air: self-amused as if aware that pukka sahibs were an endangered species.

'You'll be with us for ...?' English accent.

Anyone who could be self-amused was not completely dim, Garbo thought. Hush Puppy? Bit decrepit.

'Depends.' Garbo said and signed the register, Jeffrey Courtney.

'Business?'

'And pleasure.'

'You'll be wanting the traveller's rate.' Walton's eyes were on the guitar. Garbo let the assumption he was a travelling salesman ride. Walton bared his watch as if expecting to announce zero hour. 'We finish serving dinner in half an hour.'

'I've eaten.'

Walton pinged a bell on the reception desk.

And waited.

And waited.

'Liam!' His bellow—parade decibels—echoed through the hotel.

Suddenly, silently, Liam was there, a tall, skinny youth in joggers, jeans, white T-shirt with a bow-tie printed on it, green jacket with black facings. If he grew out to match his nose, he would be a formidable figure. He reached for the guitar case. Garbo beat him to it, leaving him to tote the duffle bag, up two flights of stairs.

The room was larger than Garbo expected with a double window on the front of the hotel. Automatically he peered through the window.

The lighted building across the street blocked the field of fire towards the war memorial on a lower level than the hotel.

The room's only storage spaces were a chest of drawers and a wall cupboard, locked and keyless. Garbo used his picklocks to open it. Old linen cupboard? Broad, deep shelves, back and both sides, rising from waist level to head height and a square ventilator grid almost filling its ceiling space.

He stowed the guitar on the highest of the back shelves, using his picklocks to re-secure the cupboard. His duffle bag he left near the chest of drawers, having taken out a towel, wet-pack and his track suit.

The bathroom was at the end of the corridor, and dry enough for spiders. But the hot-water system worked. Only after he had a bath and changed into his track suit did he notice a back-stairway leading down from the corridor.

Alternative line of retreat.

He checked it: hallway with three doors, two swing doors giving access to the kitchen and dining room, the third bolted. He eased it open. It led to a garden, beyond it the lighted A4. To his left: the coach-house back wall. He re-bolted the door and started back up the stairs. As he did, he heard from the dining-room: 'Liam, wherever you're skiving get here on the double!'

Skiving.

On the double.

At the head of the stairs, the corridor continued into an alcove. From the alcove's ceiling dangled a cord attached to a trapdoor.

Garbo was deciding on his next move when he became conscious of being eyed. He turned casually but sighted no watcher.

The bed in his room was as brassy as a bar full of blondes and twanged like a slack harp as he got under its blankets and top quilt.

He awoke once, alerted by a sound from the door. He did not get out of bed. He knew that the chest of drawers, he'd moved across the door would hold it against anything short of a battering ram. He was a mercenary operating in bandit country. He expected the natives to be hostile.

When Irish eyes are smiling, he thought, they may also be measuring you for your coffin.

The sound of a gong woke him. It took him a bewildered second—and a glance at his Seamaster: 08.00—to work out what the sound meant.

Breakfast.

He was tempted to ignore the gong. Yet if he did, he might arouse suspicion. Not only that: he needed to know more about the hotel: Walton and Liam. Other staff. Other guests.

There were other guests in the dining room, four of them like the number of chafing dishes on the sideboard: eggs fried, eggs scrambled, bacon, sausages. Toylike breakfast cereal packages. Jugs of milk and orange juice. Percolator of coffee. Pot of tea. Electric toaster.

No separate tables. One long board with a white linen tablecloth starched as stiff as the board, heavy silver plate cutlery and silver plate rings with linen napkins in them.

Garbo took his tray of scrambled eggs, bacon, sausages, toast and tea to a place near the turf fire that, on a narrow front, was holding the chill at bay. Down the table from him were an old man and an old woman who despite the contrast in their clothes—sombre suit, bright green dress—had synchronised tremors, nodding and bobbing silently to each other as they picked at their food. With them was a middle-aged man—son? nurse?—who kept putting up gentle conversational lobs—weather, television, friends—which they refused to return: a pair of ancient kids playing by their own mad rules.

Diagonally across the table from Garbo was a guy with a droopy moustache who, having finished his cornflakes, introduced himself as Trevor Rackner and said: 'Understand we're fellow travellers so to speak.'

'Understand?'

'I'm in ethical pharmaceuticals myself, and the manager here—what's his name?—said you were a traveller as well.'

What's his name? Nice vague touch. Hush Puppy? Garbo wondered and said: 'Ethical pharmaceuticals?'

'Contraceptives.'

'Spuds?'

'What've spuds got to do with it?'

'Potato blight. I thought the Irish might have had enough of birth control with that. Two million dead in the potato famine. The dead don't beget. Isn't that contraception?'

Rackner's moustache went even droopier. 'You're being facile. Still if you travel in guitars, I suppose the world can appear simple.'

Garbo wasn't very good at laughter, real or phoney. He did do a convincing line in amused indignation. 'You've got me wrong. I'm not a traveller in guitars or anything else. I'm a developer assessing various hotels here in terms of their potential to fit into a total-concept venture.'

Rackner concentrated on his fried eggs while working out his next line of approach.It wasn't subtle. 'Sounds interesting,' he said. 'Very interesting.'

'Moreish these eggs.' Garbo got up from the table and helped himself to seconds. He heaped the eggs on a slice of buttered toast and munched.

'Total-concept venture,' Rackner said.

'Diasporas, Irish and Jewish, two of the most significant happenings in history—the Jewish result of the policies of the Roman Empire, the Irish result of the policies of the British Empire.' He wiped egg from his mouth, seemingly having forgotten his point.

Rackner hadn't. 'Your point?' he said. Garbo kept eating. Rackner said: 'Anyway good luck.'

'Luck's got nothing to do with it.' Garbo was now an obsessive, angered by the obtuseness of a dope. 'I told you it was a total-concept venture. Family tree. A chain of hotels dedicated to assisting the Irish of the diaspora to trace their roots. Maps of clan territories. Clan names in Erse and English. Resident genealogist.'

'Your concept?'

'Give me a break. If it were mine, would I be here? The concept's no more mine than the finance is.' As if realising he might've said too much. 'That's in confidence, of course.'

'Absolutely.'

Garbo lowered his voice. 'Stayed at the Gresham in Dublin and the management didn't know what I was up to. Wouldn't want the management here or anywhere else to know. Could drive the price up.'

Rackner rose from the table. 'Trust me,' he said.

About as far as I can throw you by your big toe, Garbo thought, as Rackner left the dining room by its main doorway which gave onto the reception area. Garbo left by the door leading to the backstairs. He pushed open the kitchen door. Liam was there.

He did not see Garbo. He was too busy defending himself against a red-faced woman who was swiping him with her shoe. 'How many times?' A swipe. 'How many times?' Another swipe. 'How many times do I have to tell you not to shout at me.' Three swipes. 'And you with your mouth full of the food I've cooked.' Three more swipes. 'Spraying it over me. My own food.' A final swipe.

In the alcove at the head of the stairs, Garbo tugged on the dangling cord. The trapdoor tilted and he glimpsed the treads of a foldaway stair.

Enough.

At the far end of the corridor, a chambermaid emerged from a room.

His.

Bed made, towel and track-suit folded, wet-pack placed neatly on the chest of drawers and his duffle bag laid alongside it on the floor. The bitten sliver of fingernail he'd placed between the edge of the cupboard door and the lintel was still in place.

Garbo's further reconn of his theatre of operation was no more reassuring than the preliminary. The dress-circle buildings were definitely out—unless he was ready to die after getting off his killing shots.

The same factor applied to the local church spires, obvious sniper points. In fact, on the day, like the local castle, they would probably be manned by counter-snipers.

The Presbyterian Church was closed though presumably it would be open on the day. The Catholic Church was open. Garbo went in. Not many present: women mostly, children and men decreasing and increasing as from a constant, hidden spring.

On the altar a port-red lamp glowed and candles flickered golden in front of statues. Garbo drifted towards an iron-bound door at the back of the church, reckoning it must lead to a spire. Not that he expected to use it on the day. Just get an idea of the elevation and the field of fire.

Maybe spot a definite position.

'If it's confession you're after, I'll be hearing presently.' Garbo halted, confused at the priest's approach. Old guy: teeth on him that could've been made from the same plastic as his dog collar.

'Or reconciliation if you prefer.' Like someone offering a choice of dishes to a recalcitrant guest.

'Just having a squiz.'

'Ah, tourist. You mustn't miss Portora Royal School. It claims Oscar Wilde and Sam Beckett as old boys. I like to think they may have found inspiration here.'

'Is that right?'

'Everyone remembers Lady Bracknell's handbag line.'

Garbo, didn't and kept moving doorwards. The priest was saying. 'Who remembers Oscar's lines from *The Ballad of Reading Gaol*? He fronted Garbo.

'For who can say by what strange way,

'Christ brings His will to light …'

Garbo sensed he wasn't the first to be bailed up. The priest was going on: 'And then there's Beckett's perception of the thieves crucified with Christ: one condemned—do not presume; one saved—do not despair.'

Garbo faked a left, and went right past the priest. Like a cop, the priest: you have the right to remain silent, anything you say may be used in evidence at your trial.

Stupid to approach the church. Bloody stupid. He might as well have gone to the Police Training Centre and asked if they had any maps pin-pointing sniper positions.

Walking back to his hotel, he felt a twinge.

Deadline belly.

Six shitting days to go.

Time to stop doing dopey dog—otherwise he'd be putting his paws over his eyes and going to sleep. He recapped.

Phase One: Infiltration. Complete.

Phase Two: Execution. Incomplete.

Phase Three: Ex-filtration. Incomplete.

Stalemate on Phase Two.

And he had to re-contact Jessop re the markers which would also allow rehearsal of Phase Three.

– 38 –

Goliath, Belfast

Through his Nikon Jack Birton framed the Puma helicopter flying below him, its rotors slicing the grey rain into brilliant circles as it patrolled the docks area along the line of the River Lagan.

He was three hundred feet up in one of the driving cabs of the twin gantry cranes—Goliath and Samson—in Harland and Wolff's shipyard. He switched to a long lens. Beyond the shipyard and the docks was the city, its church steeples all pointing heavenwards though their pulpits might disagree on how to get there.

Connie's doing: pre-arranging the crane as the best spot from which to get possible master-shots for his picture spread. What an editor. She'd also pre-arranged for him to stay at the Helga Lodge Hotel in Cromwell Road, each of its rooms with an automatic tea-maker. Birton's own taste ran to room fridges, and he wondered at the frugality of a woman so generous in bed.

For a moment, gazing at the tea-maker, he'd been tempted by the memory of the the Europa's second-floor bar. People he'd worked with, and against, were bound to be there. So was not so-simple Simon Delamere. The last thing Birton wanted was to get loose-mouthed, and have Delamere trailing him south to Enniskillen and the jackpot shot.

Jinx. Birton didn't want to believe Delamere was his. More like he was Delamere's luck. He fell. Delamere rose: Associate Editor, Foreign Features, with an ex-officio punditry column.

It would be just like Delamere to get a fantastic shot with his foolproof Olympus.

Or a box-Brownie.

Down from Goliath Birton haunted the city for his own shots, knocking them off more or less discreetly: Elston Street, the Orange Lodge HQ with its statue of King Billy on horseback waving a sword.

Roaring armoured cars. Clattering helicopters. Chattering women. Laughing children at play. Infantrymen darting and whirling on street patrol as if they, too, were playing childhood games with weapons that were not toys.

Divis Tower rising from its attendant apartment blocks, its top-floor windows dark-visored, its flat roof crowned with surveillance aerials. Birton had spent his childhood in a similar dank tower in East London. Poxy architects never lived in them.

The Stormont Parliament, grey and magnificent on the crest of a grand sweep of lawn.

The Belfast High Court, defended by machine gun posts, and directly opposite through tunnels, Crumlin Road Jail, the Maze where he got a fresh wall poster:

So I'll wear no convict's uniform
Nor meekly serve my time
That Britain might brand Ireland's fight
Eight hundred years of crime.

Two even trickier shots: the Ulster Defence Association headquarters in Gawn Street off Newtonwards Road and Sein Fein headquarters on Sevastopol Street and the Falls Road.

The graffiti of the Shankill Road: the Red Hand of Ulster inset in the Union Jack, *God Save Our Queen, One Crown. One Faith.*

On the Falls Road: *Provos Rule! Touts will be Shot. Brits Out.*

On the Peace Line—cinder blocks, corrugated iron and razor

wire—he found a fresh spray-can scrawl:

Pipers, play me one tune,
On Scotland's wild pipes
And Ireland's,
One tune, pipers,
A strathspey and a jig,
To make a reel
That returns us to our common glories.
And one lament play, pipers,
To let our dead know,
That we, like them, are joined
In the name of the One brought low,
Who rose again for us.

There were other shots—shots of the one thing done better here—more defiantly, more resolutely—than anywhere else in the world.

Funerals.

One gave him his master shot: a father carrying a child's white coffin as if it were the proudest thing he'd ever done.

– 39 –

Lochgilphead, Argyll

Bitter the day, yet John Archie Allison was fair melted with embarrassment. On top of that, Superintendent Angus McMaster dripped sarcasm strong enough to strip the bristles from a pig.

He was leaning forward over his desk. 'To sum up, you're telling me, constable, that Detective Inspector Alec Kelvin hasn't acted on information you gave him.'

'No sir. I never said that. It's just…' Allison knew he was being hung for a lamb. He went for the sheep. 'The fact of the matter is I rang New Scotland Yard before coming to see you.'

'Oh, you rang New Scotland Yard, did you? Well, I never thought much of old Scotland Yard, I can tell you, nor the Bow Street Runners. Thieves turned thief-takers, the lot of them.'

'I rang to find out what was happening and the thing is—.'

'The thing is, as I understand it, what we're discussing took place up here not down there.'

'What I'm trying to say, sir, is Inspector Kelvin's not due to start at Scotland Yard until the fifteenth.'

McMaster swung his desk calendar round so that it faced Allison. 'Can you read? November. And today's the tenth. So what's the rush.'

'It's not exactly a rush.'

'I know that. Didn't you tell me a minute ago Inspector Kelvin said he would contact you if the passport check turned up anything.'

'He didn't.'

'Which surely means there wasn't anything.'

'It's just I've—.'

'Not again. Not the feeling you've got. Not the smell of rifle oil. We've all had a whiff of rifle oil. Do we let it go to our head? You said yourself this Courtney fellow lived down south. It was yourself who said he sailed south.'

'He was a hard case, sir. Polite enough but a right hard case.' Neither McMaster nor Allison was exactly a soft case.

'So he's bomb-proof,' McMaster said. 'You can't arrest a man for that.'

'The feeling I've got's so strong.'

'God, man. You'll be telling me next you're the seventh son of a seventh son and you had a vision.'

'No, sir. Just the feeling—the terrible feeling—the kind you have when the sergeant yells, "Outside with your rifles".'

McMaster had yelled the order in his time. He eased up on the sarcasm. 'The passport number. Let me have it. I'll see what I can do.' Allison did not speak—could not. McMaster said: 'Have you been struck dumb? Or what?' Allison remained silent. 'You're not telling me, you haven't got it?' McMaster said.

Then he, too, was struck dumb. Yet Allison could hear what McMaster was going to say when he regained his speech. He was going to say the name Moira Rankin. And Allison had a feeling about her he wasn't going to share with McMaster or anyone. 'I'm sorry, sir,' he said. 'Inspector Kelvin was in charge.'

'Exactly what I've been trying to get through to you. Listen, if you're still obsessed with the smell of rifle oil, give him a call at Scotland Yard on the fifteenth.' McMaster stood up. 'An authorised call.'

McMaster liked things regimental. Allison had been standing

throughout. He put on his uniform cap, saluted, about turned and marched out.

Relief cooled his sweat. If Moira Rankin's name had come up, McMaster might've started putting one and one together. Allison had. He'd tried to contact Moira Rankin only to be told she was on leave. It was then he'd got this feeling: that she and Kelvin were together.

That couldn't be. Not Kelvin, a toe-rag. Allison came out into the street shrugging on his heavy-duty jacket. The wind was from the north, from the mountains, from the snow and ice. Moira Rankin had held him there. Belayed him—alpenstock shaft spike driven into the snow and ice, turn of the rope round the shaft and her strength—belayed him when he slipped and preventing him from falling.

Routine.

Yet he was hers—though she might not be his.

Maybe he had too many feelings. She could never be Kelvin's. His feeling about that was wrong. Had to be. So his other feelings could be wrong as well.

It was just that the terrible feeling he remembered from the days of, 'Outside with your rifles' was connected to someone definitely getting hit.

– 40 –

Quirk's Hotel, Enniskillen

Aran-knit cardigan, Tattersall check shirt, Paisley pattern cravat and washed-out tan corduroys, Robert Walton's costume change did not alter his self-amused air while his remarks though languid were pointed.

'Nice to have you back,' he said.

'Best place in town.'

'Good trip?'

'Couldn't've been better.' Garbo meant this. His ex-filtration rehearsal had been designed to sort out his options. First option: long withdrawal north to Belfast by car and from Belfast to Dublin by train. Second option: short dash south through one of the near border areas which made Fermanagh such a madness, a salient created in haste and repented at bloody leisure. He'd decided on the first option.

'Stayed at the Europa, I suppose.' Walton handed Garbo his room key.

'Wellington Park Hotel.'

'Lots of potential for your concept.'

Garbo retained his poker face: he'd been spot on. Rackner had ben a Hush Puppy and briefed Walton. 'Yeah,' he said. 'Nice and close to the university. Despite that, give me the Old Inn out at Crawfordsburn. Thatched roof. Period furniture. Lough views. Even more potential. Almost as much as this place.' Garbo moved towards the stairs. 'Family owned, I gather.'

'Correct. Kevin Quirk runs it on behalf of his parents. You may have seen them together in the dining room.'

'Is he in?'

'Away on business.'

'The parents. Any chance of talking to them?'

'No shortage of chances. Not much point though. He's ga and she's ga which makes the pair of them gaga. As for Kevin, I could let him know you're interested in talking to him.'

'Do that.'

Garbo had no doubt Walton would first phone the Wellington Park and Old Inn, as he'd already phoned the Gresham in Dublin, to establish whether one Jeffrey Courtney had been a guest.

The dinner gong sounded as Garbo examined the guitar in the linen cupboard. A OK. He couldn't've risked another Brit squaddie wanting to buy it or pick at its strings. He re-secured the cupboard door and put into the chest of drawers a couple of denim shirts he'd bought in Belfast's security-cage shopping centre.

Belfast, he'd re-contacted Jessop. Short and showbiz: he had the markers. This and the success of his ex-filtration rehearsal had re-focused him on his main phase: Execution.

From his duffle bag, he took a gift-wrapped package and opened it to reveal the only military equipment available over the counter in Northern Ireland: a Victorinox Swiss Army knife and torch.

The knife and torch he slipped into the pocket of the Irish thornproof tweed jacket he'd also bought in Belfast. Plus a new pair of gloves.

The sound of the dinner gong had ceased. The corridor was empty. Garbo walked to the alcove. The dangling cord was still in place. He reached up for it. Again he was conscious of being eyed. Swiftly he moved to the backstairs and halfway down them. The swing door to the dining room was still moving. He retraced his steps. When he reached the alcove area, he crouched down and felt the corridor carpet. There was a slight bulge towards the centre.

Pressure alarm.

In the dining room, Robert Walton was presiding as carver and helped Garbo to roast pork, crackling, apple sauce and spuds.

The old couple were already into their synchronised bobbing, dipping and picking. Walton introduced them to Garbo; they nodded without interrupting their eating. No sign of Hush Puppy Rackner.

The far corner of the room was furnished with a wine rack. Garbo needed to present a more relaxed face. He asked about the wine. 'French, German, Italian, Spanish,' Walton said. 'You may prefer the Australian—Irish-Australian. McGuigan Brothers.'

Garbo chose a bottle of *Night Harvest Graves.* The label said: *Saint Francis Xavier, Patron Saint of Australia.* The things you didn't know. Walton opened the bottle and thrust it into a full ice-bucket. Garbo offered him a glass which he accepted. Colonel with a subaltern. The remainder Garbo drank with his roast pork and bread-and-butter pudding. Connoisseur. He held his glass by the stem, twirling it.

'Great.' Using his napkin, Garbo upended the bottle and twisted it down among the ice-cubes in the bucket. 'Okay, I take a bottle to my room?'

'Help yourself.' Walton proffered his bottle opener. Garbo held up his Swiss Army knife with its corkscrew: souse who was always prepared. A squad of what Garbo took to be rugby players erupted into the dining room. Their boisterousness, he noted, had an edge of respect when Walton gestured with his carving knife to where he wanted them to sit.

In his room, Garbo pulled on his new gloves before opening the bottle. *Night Harvest Graves.* No glass. Not to worry. No souse like a souse who drinks from the bottle. He poured most of the wine down the sink and left the dregs on the TV set after wiping the bottle with his gloved hands. The TV set he switched on: a souse inflicting on himself a double dose of brain-rot. He locked the door and barred it with the chest of drawers.

The cupboard door opened to his picklocks. He straddle-climbed on the shelves till he could reach the ventilator. Four screws. Using the Swiss Army knife he undid them and pushed the ventilator carefully into the roof space, following it himself.

His torch beam probed the darkness as he stepped from rafter to rafter, noting the fibre-glass insulation pads laid between them. Midway in the roof space, the hotel's main chimney rose high to the roof ridge and penetrated it. Beside the chimney was the main water tank, cylindrical, insulated and rising two thirds of the way up the chimney.

Beyond the chimney industrial-ply planks were laid over the rafters. On these were stored tea-chests, most of them piled to the nearside of the stairway access point. Garbo glanced at a few of the books in the tea-chests: Burke's *Speeches and Letters on American Affairs,* Aristotle's A *Treatise on Government,* Belloc's *The Servile State,* Trollope's *The Way We Live Now,* Joyce's *Ulysses,* O'Flaherty's *Famine,* Buchan's *Huntingtower* and Chesterton's *The Flying Inn.*

Garbo moved to the front slope of the roof, its slates nail-fastened to cross-laths He levered a single slate free, switched off his torch and eased the slate down.

The moon had risen. And he thought he saw—pale as a skull—the tip of the war memorial cross. He could not be sure.

Not sure at all.

'Easy now, lads.'

Scots accent. It could've been the ghost of his father so quietly had the speaker entered the roof space. And the folding stairway had made no sound.

Garbo froze in position. He could see nothing; he could hear men humping loads into the roof space. Muttered 'Fucks' and paradoxically polite 'Do you minds?'

The dining room squad. Definitely a squad. But not a rugby squad.

He waited an hour by his Seamaster before he dared move. His first action was to double check what he'd seen. It was the tip of the war memorial. His position was off to one side of it and he would need head-on shots if possible.

When he moved from behind the chimney and the water tank and saw the new boxes by the light of his torch—long, reinforced, pinewood—he did not really need to have a second look at the tea-chests. He did. Beneath the top layer of books were pistols, some silenced, SMGs, ammo magazines and grenades. He tried a nine milly Browning. He gripped the knurled slide to work the action. It was fast, oiled. No need to examine the new boxes. Unmistakably, they contained rifles.

Back in his room, he poured the dregs of the good wine down the sink and was about to switch off the television set when something about the quality of the light in the scene held him.

An impressive gent in a posh black tailcoat was leading a brace of similar guys towards the camera. The commentator was burbling on about the president of the Australian Funeral Directors Association and his well-known funeral parlours in Adelaide.

Shit, Garbo thought. Not a commercial for a funeral undertaker's business. Then he realised that he was watching: the burial of Australia's Unknown Soldier.

Australia!

Couldn't even bury its Unknown Soldier without a plug for the undertakers. He hated it.

And loved it.

Yet it was the hate he needed to complete Phase Two: Execution.

Hate and cunning.

He'd landed in the middle of someone else's operation. Inevitable, given that he was in a bandit cockpit. What he now had to decide—fast—was whether he could use the other operation to his own advantage—operate inside it, use it as camouflage.

Go!

Into the roof space this time, he carried the L42A1, freed from its guitar disguise, butt locked into firing position, load checked, safety on. He made his way to the water tank and climbed up the inspection ladder welded to its side. Under its insulation the top of the tank had a lid, a saggy lid.

He fetched a couple of the industrial-ply planks and laid them across the tank lid. Stretched on the planks, he was able to reach a line of slates higher than the one he'd already tested. This time he cut through a lath at two points so that he was able to slide three of the slates down.

He peered through the slit he'd made.

Beaut.

Dawn breaking.

A curtain of rain drifting across his theatre stage. He assumed the prone firing position, arm braced against the L42A1 rifle's sling, its muzzle inside the slit. Range: 1000.

Outside the return-fire range of any automatic rifle. Not that he expected any. Life and death were not a Western as they knew in Dallas, Texas where they were still arguing about the number and direction of

Kennedy assassination shots. He expected to fire only three. It would be a quick eye and ear that could gauge their direction.

He slid the slate shutter back into position.

The L42A1 he took with him and left it with the guitar in the cupboard before re-securing it.

The gong sounded through out the hotel. The condemned man ate a hearty breakfast, Garbo thought. The executioner? Garbo grinned. He could eat a horse.

– 41 –

Ormeau Avenue, Belfast

Looking at himself, Michael MacLirr did not like what he saw. Had the self-image before him been in a mirror, he would have fisted—headbutted—it to bloody shards. But the self-image was a hooded man, Liam Flynn, a tout, an informer, brought in the back of a van for assessment.

And aggravation: Pamela Fitzgibbon was sitting in, her Arpège mixing with the reek of Flynn's fear.

A tout of the trickiest kind, Flynn: turned by Brit intelligence jail threats to work as a Fed—a member of a Military Reconnaissance Force—under the control of a plainclothes Field Intelligence Officer.

Now the self-same tout was seeking to prove he'd turned back by revealing details of a Brit operation involving a cache of weapons in the roof space of an hotel.

MacLirr was sitting knee to knee with Flynn. Pamela Fitzgibbon was behind Flynn so that she was looking at MacLirr as he took Flynn back through his story. 'So there you are at Quirk's in Enniskillen, you say, and your guardian angel's got you in shit up to your nostrils on an operation which will involve the discovery of an arms cache.'

Flynn's voice came muffled by the hood. 'It's the Brit's own arms cache, I'm telling you. A nice wee triumph for them when they discover it, d'ye see?'

MacLirr did. He also saw that the location Enniskillen had been chosen with care. The bomb there, November 8, 1987 bad: eleven immediate, dead, sixty-three wounded. Remembrance Day service. Discovering an arms cache would revive memories of the bomb and avenge it.

'We're talking a real haul: pistols, SMGs, rifles, grenades,' Flynn was saying. 'No problems. None at all, pressure-pad alarm system you can dance around.'

'Your guardian angel? Can we dance around him?'

'I told you. He's an older guy. Robert Walton.'

'Hush Puppy?'

'Retread.'

'Retread?'

'Retired Army Officer Re-employed.'

Pamela Fitzgibbon shook her head: no questions. MacLirr considered the implications of Walton's being a Retread. Back in the Seventies, MI6, foreign section of the Secret Intelligence Service, had resented losing control of Military Reconnaissance Force operations to MI5, domestic section. What a bloody cock-up. MI5's worst. Ten Freds eliminated. Could MI5 be back with a Retread sideshow. Or was it an M15 show?

'All right,' MacLirr said. 'Let's suppose you're onto something.'

'I thought—.'

'You thought. Tell me what you thought while you still can.'

'I thought you—we—might already have someone sniffing around there.'

MacLirr laughed. 'A true, reformed turncoat. You're covering your arse.'

'On my mother's grave.'

MacLirr's blow rattled Flynn's teeth. 'On your own.'

Flynn was shaking as he told MacLirr about the guest called Jeffrey

Courtney and his story of working on a project called Family Tree. 'Walton believes him. Past it, Walton. This gink came in from the South. Stayed in Dublin, the Gresham, then up here, the Wellington Park and the Old Inn.'

'What made you suss him?'

'Funny accent,' Flynn said. 'Didn't sound natural. And the hardness.'

MacLirr motioned to the volunteer who stood by the door. He unbolted the door. Another volunteer who'd been on guard outside came in. 'Give him a bite to eat,' MacLirr said.

The volunteer had to help Flynn from the room. Of necessity MacLirr kept his intelligence data in his head. The name Jeffrey Courtney was there: sailed into Arklow, County Wicklow on a business-pleasure trip. Now in an Enniskillen hotel where the Brits appeared to be setting up a sting operation.

MacLirr waited for Pamela Fitzgibbon to speak. She did not, sitting in silence as if back at her convent, compelling him to say: 'Convincing enough, I thought.'

'Iffy. Arms cache, yes. For it to work, there've got to be perpetrators. Red-handed perpetrators. Guns plus bodies.'

MacLirr started for the door. 'You mean that pishrogue tout ... He's dead meat—setting us up for ambush if we go in after the guns.'

Pamela Fitzgibbon's cool voice halted him. 'We don't know that. We do know they've baited traps with a gun or two before.'

'And bagged good men.'

'Indeed. So let's bait them as they're baiting us. Discuss options with our man Liam. Send him back with the options, telling him for his own information as it were that we're dubious about the quality of the arms and want to inspect them.'

'Under our man's guidance?'

'We seem to trust him. Keen but not that keen. Sooner we inspect the arms, sooner we go in after them.'

'Date?'

'Dates. One for the Brits. One for ourselves.'

'We go in earlier?'

'Later, after they've had that terrible feeling, they gave a party a nobody came.'

'Okay. Dates?'

'Today's November tenth. We tell our man we're going in ... Let's say, the twenty third. Time: three a.m.'

'Real date?'

'November, 13.'

'Too close to November 11.'

'Superstitious? You?'

'Make it 15. And I do the inspection.'

'My idea. My job.'

MacLirr smiled. Not admiration. Appraisal. What a prize. She was raising her value every move she made. 'This Courtney,' he said. 'Obviously, he's not one of ours and it doesn't look as if he's one of theirs.'

'You think he's genuine?'

'Some people are. Don't worry though, I'll run a check on him.'

Some people were genuine, Pamela Fitzgibbon thought. A few. And Michael MacLirr was not one of them.

– 42 –

Cenotaph, London

Impeccably turned out in black, Rex D'Acre braced himself as Big Ben tolled.

One

First stroke of the eleventh hour, the slow reverberation sounding through the city and beyond to tell the world Great Britain was remembering its war dead on this, the first Sunday after the eleventh day of the eleventh month. He was with the Royal Household, an élite without its most superb couple, H.R.H. Prince Charles and H.R.H. the Princess Diana, separated to avoid petty embarrassment during the remembrance of manifold sacrifice.

Naturally, D'Acre's felt disappointed at his exclusion from the prince's entourage for the Arab Gulf states trade mission. This, however, was the place and time to confront what he'd set in train. He fingered the mobile phone in his overcoat pocket as if it were an amulet.

In the ranks of the Guards Division, he glimpsed Guy Jessop, bowler hat, dark great coat, rapier-rolled black umbrella. D'Acre was in awe of Jessop and the metallic voice on the telephone. Such subtle caution betokened the need to protect an ultimate secret.

Agenda One.

Agenda One—dedicated to the defence of the Monarchy and the

Realm at all hazard—was with him.

Sublime Prince of the Royal Secret.

Quirk's Hotel, Enniskillen.

Two

The television set in Garbo's room was tuned to the London remembrance service. Garbo himself was above it on the water tank, totally focused through the L42A1 sight on the local memorial, 1000 yards from his position.

Flags streaming at half-mast, his windage.

His markers: red on black.

Bloke in a red and black cap.

And another in a similar cap.

The third red-on-black: no cap, big black hat, beneath it three red poppies on the black lapel of an elegant coat.

The face under the big, black hat, he knew. Who did not?

Firing time: 11.00 hours. He eased the slate shutter down over his aiming slit. No point in exposing his position to the possibility of being spotted.

Ocean Drummer, Arklow.

Three

Leaving one volunteer in the dinghy and another on the quay, Michael MacLirr clambered on board the ketch. He ducked out of the rain under the blue tarp, spread across the cockpit. He had come prepared. His bolt-cutter sheared through the below-decks padlock.

He'd told Pamela Fitzgibbon he would run a check on Jeffrey Courtney. What he hadn't told her was that it was more of an alibi for himself than a check. He prowled through the boat. Well-found. Stocked for a long voyage: everything from beans mean O'Reilly shites gold to shortbread in a tartan tin with the portrait of a Highlander on it. He was tempted to sample its contents. More than shortbread was coming his way when Sister Pam was found with the arms cache and copped the blame while M15, MI6, the Hush Puppies got the applause with the RUC Special Branch trying to edge into the picture.

War Memorial, Enniskillen.

Four

Reporters Jack Birton considered to be retarded adolescents. The more promotion they got, the more retarded they seemed to become. Not-so-simple Simon Delamere was the worst of them—an orang-outang who'd learned to tie a Windsor knot. He kept tugging at his red and black cap and trying to snatch Birton's.

'Cock-a-doodle-do!'

The rest of the pack were pissing themselves laughing at this by-play, all the funnier since it was taking place surreptitiously amid solemnity and the intense snap and whirr of cameras like some other kind of musketry.

Quirk's Hotel, Enniskillen.

Five

For most of his life, Robert Walton had been taking and giving orders as well as enduring changes in command. Neither had prepared him for Briony Leonard, a brunette, up the duff, charming with it, needing a room and looking at him as if she wished he were the father.

He thanked his lucky stars that a one-night stand couple had come—so to speak—and gone, and determined to protect her from Jeffrey Courtney who appeared to be finding more and more inspiration in McGuigan Brothers Night Harvest Graves.

Lochgilphead, Argyll.

Six

Dialling Inspector Alec Kelvin's London home number. Constable John Archie Allison was nervous, more as a result of his meeting with Moira Rankin from whom he'd got the number than anticipation of Kelvin's reaction.

'Courtney?' he said.

Allison shouted: 'Jeffrey Courtney—the fellow we questioned. You were going to check his passport.'

'Oh, him. Don't worry. Don't worry. I'll see you get your due credit.'

'Credit?

'Stolen passport. One of five blanks. As from tomorrow, your Mr. Courtney will have the Met on his tail.'

'Ah, *Dhia, Dhia*.' Not idle blasphemy. A desperate prayer. Allison had been re-galvanised into action early that morning after being called out to inspect the carcass of a stag, washed out of the deep pool by a spate.

And with it, the antlered head used to kill the gamekeeper.

'Dhia,' he said again. Kelvin wasn't into Gaelic. He hung up. Allison yelled into the dead phone: 'Tomorrow will be too late.'

Quirk's Hotel, Enniskillen

Seven

Slate shutter down, Garbo sighted on the stage of his theatre. He bolted the first killing round into the breech of the L42A1—cock, dock, lock—loud in the roof space.

His ex-filtration phase was as clear and certain as his target: abandon the L42A1 among the other weapons, cache the guitar beneath the roof insulation, easy drive to Belfast, train Dublin and then onto his boat for a long voyage.

Ocean Drummer, Arklow.

Eight

No worry. No hurry. Michael MacLirr'd decided Jeffrey Courtney was clean. Yet the longer he spent on board, the more vivid his own get-away dream became.

He finished examining the boat's sat-nav equipment and moved toward the auxiliary engine. One day, given his payment from Delamere's newspaper, he would be able to afford such a boat. His sweetener from M15 would enable him to run the boat.

They'd practically been coming in their pants instead of their hands which was their usual—wankers. An entrancing prospect, right enough: winning the confidence of Pamela Fitzgibbon, Buckingham Palace spy, by allowing her to nominate the arms-cache inspection date—November 13—and then lifting her when she returned with a party to seize the arms.

He had been using a jiggle-key to unlock the engine. He pressed the starter button. The blast from the block of Composition 4, Garbo'd wired to the engine was so quick, so powerful, so all encompassing that Michael MacLirr was dead before he could finish calculating how much extra he could ask Simon Delamere for the full story.

Cenotaph, London.

Nine

In the booming silence, Rex D'Acre had an impulse to cry out his plot. Yet he knew he could no more halt it than he could roll back history to stop Charles I—sold by the Scots, condemned by the English—stepping onto the high scaffold in front of the Banqueting House further along Whitehall to be executed, wearing two shirts to prevent a shiver of cold being mistaken for cowardice.

The memory of that kingly, that cathartic end had inspired the restoration of the monarchy after Cromwell's death. Little kingliness, less catharsis in the present Windsor black farce.

Necessary restoration: Charles III, through the Princess Diana! She of the myriad images, mediated worldwide: wilful, beguiling, gawky, elegant, compassionate, brave and always beautiful, would have a new image.

Diana.

Dear departed.

Immortal pop icon.

An image to complement Charles, the Widower of Windsor with his companion Camilla Parker-Bowles, as potent a monarch as his great-great-great grandmother, Victoria, Widow of Windsor with her companion, John Brown.

Madness and its certainty seized Rex D'Acre: his plan accorded with the secret consensus of Agenda One. And he knew he had been correct to get the completion payment ready in cash.

Success—never failure—success was his.

Sublime Prince of the Royal Secret.

War Memorial, Enniskillen.

Ten

Shot of his life: Jack Birton knew it was his, the shot Rex D'Acre wanted, the shot that would remind Charlie Chester what Di really meant to him.

Never more radiant.

More entrancing.

More serene.

Black hat. Black coat. Three red poppies in a shamrock shape on her lapel.

Pearls at her throat and ears. He was sure he'd caught a tear—a more precious pearl—sliding down her pale cheek.

Got it.

Yet his hunter's instinct was still fierce. He turned to get a shot of the adoring crowd. High on the pitch of a roof, he caught a glimpse of light.

Telescopic lens? Another photog. Poxie Froggie? Keen, Froggies. Dead keen. Two could play that game. He switched to his own long lens.

Not another photog. Sniper. Birton's first impulse was to yell a warning. Amid the manic click and whirr of the pack, and their murmured entreaties to their provider, Di, he acted on his second impulse. He turned to focus his Nikon on her.

He would show that cock-a-doodle-do berk, Delamere. He would show the bleeding lot of them.

The jackpot shot.

Quirk's Hotel, Enniskillen.

Eleven

Garbo drew in a breath and took first pressure on the L42A1 trigger. He half exhaled, the No. 32 sight eye-locked to him by his gloved hands and the taut rifle sling. The face of the target was in the cross-hairs: mark of Cain.

Breathing her last.

Flower.

Woman.

Bright light.

Waiting to be put out.

His secret. Not zen. On the target—male, female, animal, vegetable, mineral—he superimposed the head of the benign bastard. This time it shifted to his own: he should've—could've—got his father out of the loony-bin.

Beside him, he heard an indrawn breath. He twisted round and for a split second thought it the supple slip of a woman, all hungry eyes, hollow cheeks and feral red hair who'd wanted to accompany him.

'No,' he said, even as he tried to kick her face.

Pamela Fitzgibbon's response was in her hand: a silenced Beretta taken from the cache when she heard Garbo bolting the killing round in.

She'd aimed to outfox MacLirr by going in early. Had he outfoxed her?

The short answer was the Beretta's .25 round. Garbo's head snapped back from its impact. She eased the L42A1 from his grip and sighted on his target …

Smiling.

Was there ever an Irish chieftain so petty, ever a high king so low as The Kight of the Garter, Knight of the Tampon, Knight of the Horns in distant parts, and his wife, mother of his children, in a place where she might be in death's sight, a place of blood: eleven killed and sixty-three wounded by a bomb. November 8, 1987.

A Sunday.

Another bloody Sunday.

The L42A1 was steady. Her enemy was in her sights: her enemy, her sister.

Her betrayed sister.

She laid the L42A1 down and closed the slit.

Jack Birton knocked off a final shot of Di leaving the Enniskillen war memorial.

'Cock-a-doodle-do!' Delamere's cry ended in a gasp as Birton's punch took him flush on the mouth. He staggered against another reporter who pushed him back towards Birton. But Birton was legging it for his car, trying to persuade himself he'd been wrong about the sniper.

His trade was images of reality. What he'd got was a great image. Was it the image Rex D'Acre was expecting? By then in his hire car, Birton suspected not. His heaving, sour spew confirmed his suspicion. There had been a sniper. No question. Yet he hadn't shouted a warning.

Not a dicky-bird.

He shared complicity with the sniper.

And with Rex D'Acre?

Silence.

Guilty silence.

A4 lay-by, Enniskillen

Rain slashed across the windscreen of Pamela Fitzgibbon's Audi and the wipers metronomed it away. No metronome, however, no music, to clear her tears. Doubtless, Hush Puppies would come into the roof space intent on lifting her. Let them make what they would of the dead man and the L42A1. She knew who he was: Rex D'Acre's ruffian hired ostensibly to chastise Scribes and Pharisees.

Diana's ruffian in waiting.

Shivers came with her tears, shivers like a soldier's come from a killing ground. And dread: plots were amoebic. One begot another: the sister she'd spared—so fair yet so forsaken—she sensed was nevertheless doomed, fated to whirl with a string of partners, mirror-images of her faithless prince, in a taunting dance, a dance of untimely death.

And for that, there was no human remedy. Pamela Fitzgibbon put the Audi in gear and turned west, not north to Belfast and the battle, as she'd intended, west towards Connemara, an abbey cell and prayer.

Alisdair Guthrie's prayer: 'Sir Jesus, forgive us all.'

Author's Note

This is a work of fiction. The Prologue replaces a structure, designed to give the fiction a documentary air by suggesting an anonymous writer, and that it came through a palace contact working in the Royal Mews (Horse's mouth. Geddit).

The fiction's point of departure, as indicated in the Prologue, was the *Who* (6/12/1993 Australian edition of America's *People*) containing a photograph of Diana Spencer, alone at the hazardous location which features in the novel.

No mention has been sighted in posthumous official inquiries and reports as to the prudence of Diana Spencer being at this a location, perhaps because the relevant date was outside terms of reference.

The narrative is as originally written except for the Prologue, and the editing required as a result of the typewritten version having to be scanned.

Acknowledgement of reliance on a number of distinguished works is a must: *Inside the Brotherhood* by Martin Short (Grafton Books); *Stalker* by John Stalker (Penguin Books); *Inside Buckingham Palace* by Andrew Morton (Michael O'Mara Books); *The Rise and Fall of the House of Windsor* by A.N. Wilson (Sinclair-Stevenson) *Who Dares Wins* by Tony Geraghty (Arms and Armour); *Soldier 'I' S.A.S.* by Michael Paul Kennedy (Bloomsbury) *Catholic Curiosities and Oddities by* Paul Stenhouse MSC, Ph.D. (Chevalier Press).

The poem quoted in the text is, *His Metrical Prayer (On the Eve of his Own Execution)* by James Graham, Marquis of Montrose (*The*

Penguin Book of Scottish Verse, editor Tom Scott).

In accumulating general background, a main source was the work of the Fleet Royal Pack with whom, long ago, I had runs.

Personal thanks are due to my wife, Jenny Pritchard Murray, our children, relatives and friends.

Professional thanks go to the eminent British publisher Christopher MacLehose who commended the original draft. Michael Wilding, Australia and Britain's most prolific academic-novelist-publisher read that draft, and secured publication through Nick Walker's Arcadia/ Australian Scholarly Publishing.

No one has equaled in impact the words of Gordon Wilson, mourning his daughter, Marie, nurse of the Royal Victoria Hospital, Belfast, killed in the Enniskillen bombing of 1987.

'I bear no ill will. That sort of talk is not going, to bring her back to life. She was a great, wee lassie. She loved her profession. She was a pet and she's dead. She's in heaven and we'll meet again. Don't ask me please for a purpose. I don't have a purpose. I don't have an answer but I know there has to be a plan. If I did not think that, I would commit suicide. It is part of a greater plan and God is good and we shall meet again.'

About the Author

In the early 1950s James Murray's first printed work appeared in what was then the *Glasgow Herald*, his native city's morning newspaper; the printing was a kind of consolation prize given to also-rans in a competition for which the prize was a Collins contract to write a novel. The winner was Alistair Maclean whose novel *H.M.S. Ulysses* remains the greatest written about World War II sea warfare, though paradoxically overshadowed by his subsequent thrillers.

Murray used his first cuttings to take passage into journalism, including ten years mainly with the *Daily Mirror* (Manchester and London) pre- and post the Rupert Murdoch era. Balancing experience in Australia included the *Sun News-Pictorial*, *Australian Women's Weekly*, *National Times*, and *Sydney City Monthly Magazine*. His introduction to Australian journalism was through the *Young Australian* in Adelaide, a children's comic-cum-newspaper; he notes that it was perhaps the most serious a publication he has worked on.

His first fiction, a short story, 'Rafferty Resting', appeared in the *Bulletin* (Literary Editor, Patricia Rolfe; Editor, Peter Coleman). His first novel, *The Pale Sergeant* was published after Tom Keneally gave him the name of his then agent, the irreplaceable Tessa Sayle.

Assignments in the UK and in Australia have taken Murray to continental Europe, the United States, Africa and Asia. He supports his fiction habit through film reviews and media commentary in *Annals Australasia*, and is currently re-shaping his new novel (about the end of the world as we know it) to take account of the ascendancy of President Donald John Trump. He lives in Sydney with his first and future wife, Jenny, surrounded by their children and their children's families.

Printed in Australia
AUOC02n0818310117
282614AU00008B/8/P

9 781925 333619